DiFFERENt

WHITEABBEY PRESBYTERIAN
CHURCH
602 Shore Road, Newtownabbey,
Co. Antrim, BT37 0SN
Tel: (028) 9086 4084

ELEANOR DAVIES

Copyright © Eleanor Davies 2005
First published 2005
ISBN 1 84427 090 4

Other books by the same author:
Designer Label
In the Spotlight
Halfway House

Scripture Union, 207–209 Queensway, Bletchley, Milton Keynes, MK2 2EB, England.
Email: info@scriptureunion.org.uk
Website: www.scriptureunion.org.uk

Scripture Union Australia
Locked Bag 2, Central Coast Business Centre, NSW 2252
Website: www.scriptureunion.org.au

Scripture Union USA
PO Box 987, Valley Forge, PA 19482
Website: www.scriptureunion.org

British Library Cataloguing-in-Publication Data.
A catalogue record of this book is available from the British Library.

Printed and bound in Great Britain by Creative Print and Design (Wales) Ebbw Vale

Cover design: GoBallistic Design Ltd

Scripture Union is an international Christian charity working with churches in more than 130 countries, providing resources to bring the good news about Jesus Christ to children, young people and families and to encourage them to develop spiritually through the Bible and prayer.

As well as our network of volunteers, staff and associates who run holidays, church-based events and school Christian groups, we produce a wide range of publications and support those who use our resources through training programmes.

With special thanks to Martin Hallett

One

There hadn't been so much excitement at the club since the time when Darren Brookes had thrown a firecracker into the girls' toilets.

'Hey, Eves! Come and get a load of this!'

Over the hubbub of the crowd Evie Wilson could just make out the voice of her best friend, Vicki.

She struggled past the crowd of people clustering round the noticeboard and elbowed her way through the group until she was standing next to Vicki. There in the middle of the board was the cause of all the fuss; a huge, brightly coloured new poster. It was printed on shiny paper and there was a kind of explosion of yellow light in the foreground. In the middle of the light stood the silhouette of a microphone with musical notes jumping out in all directions like a flock of birds. Printed in bold eye-catching letters, the poster's message was clear:

HAVE YOU GOT WHAT IT TAKES TO BE A STAR?

INTER-SCHOOL SINGING COMPETITION
FIRST HEAT FRIDAY 16 FEBRUARY
OPEN TO ALL SECONDARY SCHOOL PUPILS IN
STANWORTH AREA

For further details call in at your school office

Piles of flyers, scaled-down versions of the poster, lay in random heaps on surfaces round the club.

'Whose great idea is this, then?' said Evie.

'Dunno,' said Vicki. 'Maybe something the music teachers came up with after a particularly heavy night at the pub. One of their special Friday evening after-school jobs.'

'Sounds a bit different. P'raps we should ask Ben about it.' Evie looked round for the youth worker but he was nowhere to be seen.

It had been a tiring day at school. Her favourite sofa in the corner was empty and she made a beeline for it, rooting around in her school bag for the magazine she'd started reading at lunchtime. There was a quiz on the centre page called *So you think you know your friends...?* that she'd been looking forward to completing all day.

She lowered herself into the squashy depths of the sofa, fished a leaky black rollerball out of her pencil case and focused her full attention on the knotty problem of deciding whether her mate Vicki preferred a night out on the town or staying in with the girls. It all depended on what kind of mood she was in and which girls she was going to stay in with, thought Evie.

She sucked her pen and sighed. Perhaps it had been a mistake to come this evening when she was feeling so low.

Usually she loved coming to the Halfway House. Originally a pub, it had been left by the owner in his will to the young people of St Michael's Church just three years previously. With the help of the youth worker, Ben, they'd turned it into an after-school drop-in centre for local teenagers. It was a haven at the end of a hectic day at school; a place where she could go just to chill out, listen to music and be with her friends. She visited the club several nights a week on her way home and had come to know loads of people from other schools; people like Vicki and Hannah, who she would never have met any other way. Besides all the socialising the club ran lots of after-school activities: things like bowling, sailing, rock climbing, football and Evie's favourite, skating. There were Christian events too and for those who were interested, a regular meeting on Sunday evenings after church.

'Luscious lippy,' said a voice in Evie's ear. She sat up straight and looked over her shoulder. A lanky boy with light brown hair, slate-coloured eyes and a mildly spotty chin was grinning down at her.

'Adam!'

Adam was her best friend. They had always done everything together, including making their first venture into Halfway House two years ago when they had both been just 14. People who didn't know them well assumed they must be brother and sister, twins even; they were never apart. It was Adam who had helped Evie through her mother's death last year, and Adam who knew just when to talk and when to keep quiet in the difficult times. Vicki was a great mate too, but Adam was closest – perhaps because she had known him all her life.

'Julie and I were in hospital beds next to each other when you two were born,' her mother had told her. Julie was Adam's mum. 'Just one day between you. You wouldn't believe the laughs we had on that ward. None of the nurses could really believe we'd called you Adam and Eve, they all thought we were winding them up. But we'd thought of the names quite independently and neither Jules nor I would change our mind, so Adam and Eve you stayed. Very apt as it turned out later – you were always getting him into trouble when you were toddlers, just like Eve and the apple. He was such a nice thoughtful little boy. Mind, your dad would've liked a fancier name – he wanted Roxana or Olivia – but I stuck to my guns and you were baptised Eve, although in the end we've always called you Evie.'

It seemed to Evie that Adam's father hadn't had much of a say in his son's name either, but then he'd hardly hung around long enough to get to know him. Long before Adam's first birthday he had gone to live in Madrid with the Spanish exchange student who was lodging next door, leaving Julie to bring up the new baby and his 18-month-old brother, Tom, all on her own.

She smiled up at Adam. 'I thought you must have decided to go straight home. You're much later than usual.'

He dumped a jumble of bags on the floor in front of the sofa and swiped at her legs. 'Shove over, the settee's meant to be for general use. I had an extra music lesson. Mr Barraclough missed the last one and it was the only time he could make it up. What have you been doing to your face?'

'What are you on about?'

'Your mouth. It's all black. Have you gone Goth?'

'What...? Oh, it's probably this.' Evie held up her mangled rollerball for his inspection. 'Do I look really dreadful?'

'Like something from the *Rocky Horror Picture Show*. And you've got a great big hole in your tights.' He pushed her hand off the magazine in her lap and squinted at where she'd been ticking boxes.

'*So you think you know your friends?*' he read. 'Well, do you?'

''Course I do,' said Evie.

'How does it work, then? What do you have to do?'

'You've got to answer all these questions about your best friend, like who their favourite actor is and their best food and that kind of stuff. And then you get them to fill it in separately and see if you get the same answers.'

'Which friend are you doing it about? Is it me?'

'No, durrbrain, I have other friends, you know. Vicki, actually. No need to do it for you.'

'Oh, so you think you know me that well, do you?'

'Guess so. Anyway it's a girl thing.'

'Oh, silly me. So what's this learned publication called?' He whipped the magazine away from her and read out the title from the front page. '*Impressions*. Haven't seen this one before. Is it new? Are you finally going to discover the secret of how to get the guy you've always dreamed of?'

Evie snatched it back. 'Stop taking the mick. I was just passing time. Don't really believe in it. Most quizzes are a waste of space.'

'Ah, but are they? I mean, like you say you know everything about me. Bet you don't know me as well as you think you do.'

'Don't be a jerk, I've known you since I was one day old. What could I not know about you?'

He gave a sly smile. 'What's my favourite colour?'

'Green. Always has been.'

'My favourite food?'

'Curry.'

'My favourite band?'

'Escape. No, Bennett Boys. No, Randall Cooper. Except he's not a band. Anyway, that one's not fair, 'cause it changes every month.'

'But if you really knew me you'd keep up, wouldn't you?' he said triumphantly. 'Favourite sport?'

'Easy. Football.'

'OK, try this one. Who do I really fancy?'

'No one. The only person you've ever been remotely interested in was Anna Murphy and that was over a year ago. I'd be the first to know if you did fancy someone.' She looked at him closely. 'I am right, aren't I?'

An infinitesimal pause. 'Yeah, of course. You know everything. No secrets. And tell you what, I know something about you.'

'What?'

'I know why you're sitting in that chair doing that stupid quiz and looking all mopey and depressed.'

'You do?'

'Yeah, sure I do. You're remembering it's your mum's birthday today and you're missing her loads, and thinking no one cares. But I do.'

'Oh, Ad.' To her annoyance Evie found her eyes filling. 'I didn't think anyone would know.'

'Well, I do. I loved her too, you know. Those birthday dinners we used to do. Remember the one when I tried to help you make that chocolate mousse and it came out looking like a pile of...'

'Yeah, yeah, I remember,' Evie giggled. 'And we covered it with squirty cream and hoped she wouldn't notice.'

She smiled wistfully at the memory. Thinking about her mum always made her feel weird, kind of deeply happy and incredibly miserable all at once. Adam was the only person who really understood. And her dad, of course, but she couldn't talk to him about how she felt in case they both ended up crying at once, like they'd kept doing in the early days after her mum's death. If it hadn't been for Adam, she'd never have survived.

She opened her mouth to say something else but his attention had been diverted by a noisy discussion between Leo Hopkins and Darren Brookes, still lurking by the notice board.

'What's the poster?'

Evie shrugged and passed him a flyer. 'Some sort of song contest. It doesn't say much about it. Apparently there'll be more details in school.'

'Something we could do?'

'I hardly think so. What, me and you?'

'Why not? It'd be worth checking out at least, wouldn't it?'

Evie laughed. 'But Ad, you can't – um, how shall I say this nicely? – you can't sing.'

'Who said anything about singing? I'll write a song and you can sing it. Can't you just see it? Adam and Eve, the winning combination. Your magical voice and my immense musical talent. I'll write you a proper song; real words and real music. You'll be the new Madonna.'

'Forget it.'

'The new Kylie, then. Bum and all. I'm sure we could come up with something good. I know the kind of thing you're best at.'

He did, too. It wouldn't be the first time he'd written a song for her. They'd done a couple of numbers at the youth club cabaret last year. It wasn't really fair, thought Evie, the way he could not only play the guitar so well but also anything you cared to suggest on the piano completely by ear. Evie herself had a reasonable singing voice, but she wasn't in the same musical league as Adam.

'Anyway, the whole thing's bound to be a flop,' she said dismissively. 'Have you ever known Greenlands Comp and Stanworth High take part in anything together without it all dissolving into chaos? The two schools hate each other. Look at Leo and Brooksie over there. They're already fighting about which school has the greatest talent.'

'All the more reason for us to set a good example,' said Adam self-righteously. 'We're above that sort of thing.'

'Yeah, right. Just as long as someone from Stannie wins.'

'Obviously.'

Halfway House was beginning to fill up with people. It had been raining all afternoon and the youth club provided a welcome bolt-hole for those who were fed up with roaming the streets. The room was becoming warm and humid.

'I'm thirsty,' said Evie, hauling herself to her feet. 'Gonna get a drink.' She wandered over to join Vicki by the bar.

'Your usual, Evie?' smiled Ben's wife, Sue, reaching into the little fridge beneath the counter for a can of tropical Tango. Sue served behind the bar most days, dishing out drinks, crisps, words of wisdom and expressions of love in equal measures. She was a kind of second mum, especially to those who didn't have the kind of parents they could talk to.

Leo and Brooksie had stationed themselves by the open front entrance and a drift of cigarette smoke wafted into the atmosphere. Almost as if an invisible alarm button had been pressed, Ben emerged from the kitchen. 'Oi, Brooksie!' he shouted. 'No smoking in the club! How many more times am I going to tell you?'

'But it's raining outside,' whined Brooksie. He dropped the cigarette on the floor and stood on it, exhaling a steady stream of smoke. Glancing out into the street he called, 'Hey, Adam. Your big brother's out here, mate. Another bloke with him too, real cool dude. All the gear.'

'My brother here?' said Adam, 'Surely not. Must be someone else. Tom never comes down here these days. Anyway, he plays football on Wednesday evenings.'

But his brother was already through the door, shaking rain off his team sweatshirt and looking round the club.

Beside the bar Vicki nudged Evie so hard she nearly spilt her Tango. 'Evie, look! It's that guy Dave again,' she mouthed.

Behind Tom stood another boy, tall and blond, also in football kit. Real sun-streaked blond, not the brash yellow chemical kind that some of the lads at Halfway House went in for. His long brown legs were caked with dirt but he looked completely at ease, as though racing up and down a muddy pitch and kicking balls would be as effortless and natural for him as breathing.

'I'm not blind,' muttered Evie, barely moving her lips. She smiled sweetly at the two boys, while one of her vital organs (her stomach maybe? or perhaps her heart?) executed a neat somersault.

She and Vicki had first met Dave properly the previous weekend when Adam had dragged the two of them along to watch Tom play in the final of the Stanworth Under-18s League. Dave was in Tom's team and one of his best friends, but both boys went to the Sixth Form College and although Evie had seen him around and admired him from afar, she hadn't had a chance to do much more than exchange a quick smile with him. He'd talked to her after the match, drinking cokes in the club room and she'd thought he was totally drop-dead gorgeous.

And here he was now with Tom, pushing his way through the crowd to the bar and asking for Coke and crisps.

'What are you doing here?' said Evie. The question came out far more abruptly than she'd intended.

'Thought you'd be pleased to see us,' laughed Dave. 'Or do you have special rights to the place? Evie, isn't it?'

He'd remembered her name.

''Course not,' she said, 'but Tom never comes in here now. You said there were too many religious strings attached, didn't you Tom?'

'And so there are,' said Tom. 'You come in here and the next thing you know, they're trying to get you to church. Did all that when I was a kid. Don't need to do it again.'

'He came because I made him,' said Dave looking directly at her. 'After the football match last week I was hoping I – we – might see you again, and he told me you and Adam were always in here after school.'

Evie, painfully aware of the treacherous flush creeping across her face, struggled for an expression of cool indifference, but the best she could come up with was a weak 'Oh', accompanied by a silly grin. He looked extra fit standing there beside Tom. The random thought crossed her mind that if they were animals, Tom would be a big, bumbling gorilla and Dave would be a graceful golden lion, strong and agile.

Adam materialised behind her. 'Tom talking rubbish as usual?'

'He said he doesn't come here in case people talk religion to him,' said Evie, not even really thinking about what she was saying. She was still trying to take in the fact that Dave was in the club for no other reason than to see her again.

'Is that likely?' asked Dave nervously.

'Compulsory,' said Adam. He made spooky psycho noises and spoke in a deep sinister voice. 'No one leaves here till they've sold their soul. Don't say we didn't warn you.'

Dave stared at him anxiously for a moment, then said, 'Ha ha. Very funny. Tom told me this place was open to anyone.'

''Course it is,' put in Vicki quickly. 'It's just run by St Michael's. You don't have to believe in God or anything to come in here.'

'Do you believe in God, then?' said Dave, looking straight at Evie again. He had this way of looking right into her eyes which made her feel as though everything she said was terribly interesting. It was quite disconcerting.

'Yes, I do as a matter of fact,' she said rather shortly. She wasn't sure how far she wanted to pursue this conversation; it wouldn't do to be written off as a fruitcake so early in their acquaintance.

'No, really? And what about you, Adam?'

'Yeah, me too.'

'Is it just 'cause of your families?' persisted Dave. ''Cause your mum and dad do?'

'My mum's dead actually,' said Evie, then seeing Dave's immediate embarrassment felt sorry she'd been so abrupt. 'That's one of the reasons I believe in God, if you want to know. Without him I don't think I'd have got through the last two years.'

Dave looked even more embarrassed. 'Sorry I asked. Didn't mean to upset you.'

'I'm not upset. Anyway, the family thing doesn't always work. Look at Adam and Tom; their mum goes to church and always has done and Adam believes and Tom doesn't. It's a matter of your own choice.'

'It's not that I don't believe God exists, exactly,' said Tom looking a bit uncomfortable. 'It's just that he seems like a terrible killjoy. Everything you want to do turns out to be a big no-no. No booze, no wild parties, no birds, no fun. I got fed up with feeling so guilty all the time and decided it was better just to give the whole thing a miss.'

'You've got a really weird idea of what God's like,' said Adam.

But Dave had got bored with talking about God. Someone had left a flyer about the competition on the bar and he picked it up and scanned it. 'What's all this about a singing contest? Any of you guys going in for it?'

'Certainly are,' Adam said before Evie could open her mouth. 'We were just talking about it before you came in. Evie's totally up for it, aren't you, Eves? Main problem is finding a song. Any ideas?'

Dave had plenty. In no time he and Adam became embroiled in a friendly argument about which bands' songs were most adaptable for amateurs.

'If we did someone else's song it'd have to be something I could get the chords for,' said Adam. 'Either that or a backing track.'

'Are you into Delusion?' asked Dave.

'Who isn't? You have to support the local band. Anyway, I really like their music.'

'Me too,' said Dave, 'I've got all their albums except the third one.'

'Johnny Harker, the lead singer, used to live in our road,' said Adam. 'You can see his old house from my bedroom window.'

'Except he moved when he got rich,' put in Tom. 'Who'd stay here if they had pots of money?'

'Well, anyway, we can always look for backing tracks on the Internet if we haven't got anything suitable,' said Evie.

'And what about the whole act?' asked Tom. 'I mean, there's more to performing than just opening your mouth and singing. You're gonna have to plan out your whole act from start to finish.'

'Yeah, you don't want to end up looking like Ricky Gervais doing his Comic Relief number,' said Adam.

Dave chuckled. 'That was just so cool, wasn't it? Did you see the Christmas one, too?'

'You bet, I got the whole series on DVD,' said Adam. 'Funniest thing ever on telly.'

'No way. The whole series? Tom, why didn't you tell me your brother was an *Office* freak? I'll have to come round and see them all. What's your best episode?'

Once started, there was no stopping them. For the next fifteen minutes Dave and Adam launched into a re-enactment of the hundred funniest moments from *The Office*. Evie laughed politely. Personally she thought it was a fairly stupid programme, but she supposed it was worth it to sit there and be included in the conversation. It was a long time since she'd seen Adam get on so well with anyone. He tended to be quite a loner. Not that he didn't have loads of casual friends; she just didn't think he told anyone besides her what really went on in his mind. But he and Dave seemed to be completely on the same wavelength.

At last there was a brief lull in the regurgitated sketches and Vicki said quickly, 'I'm off. Homework to do. See you later.'

Tom turned to Adam, 'Game of pool? Table's free.'

All at once Evie found herself alone with Dave by the bar. Shyness suddenly overwhelmed her.

He offered her a crisp. 'Are you doing anything this weekend?'

Was he going to ask her out? Hurriedly she ran a mental check of her weekend plans. An English essay that she could fit into her free periods, and she'd promised her dad she'd do the ironing but she could do that any time. Saturday night was a bit more tricky; she and Adam usually did things together then.

'Saturday night, for instance?' Dave persisted.

'Yes. No. Nothing. I've nothing planned.'

'Do you want to come to a party, then? It's a friend's eighteenth and he's booked a room at Number Thirty-Seven. Everyone's been told to bring a friend.'

'But you've got to be 18 to go there. I'm only sixteen.'

'No worries, they relax the rules for private parties. I'm not 18 yet either.'

Evie thought swiftly. She could already hear her dad. 'But Evie, you're too young for that dive,' and 'Evie, how are you going to get home?' and 'Evie, who else will be there?' Parents could be very predictable. Never mind, deal with all that when it happened. No point in getting worked up about it now.

'That'd be great.'

'Cool. Meet you outside here, about half eight? Then we can walk up together.'

Her mobile beeped loudly. She rummaged in her blazer pocket to find it and pressed the key for her text message inbox. It was from her dad.

Where are you? What are we eating tonight? He'd only recently learned how to text and always did long, beautifully spelled messages with no mistakes. Predictive texting was completely beyond him.

She jumped to her feet. 'I gotta go. Dad's stressing. I'll see you later.'

'OK.' He grinned. 'Missing you already...'

It might not be so bad, she thought as she walked down the hill towards her bungalow. Adam'll be OK. He'll understand if I can't go round on Saturday, and anyway, there's always Sunday. I'll phone him later this evening, rather than get him to talk about it back there with everyone listening.

In the meantime she had two days to plan what to wear. She tried very hard to think calmly. After all, she and Dave hardly knew each other yet, and dazzling good looks didn't necessarily mean she had met her future soulmate.

But as she turned the corner into her own road a few minutes later there was a spring in her step.

Two

In the end Evie and her dad settled for sausages and baked potatoes for dinner. Neither of them had had time to go shopping so they had to resort to raiding the freezer. Evie didn't mind, as sausages were one of her favourite foods. There was something very comforting about the way they split open when you stuck a fork into the brown, crunchy skin and the spicy, pink meat burst out. The only things in the fridge were milk, a couple of eggs, an untouched pot of extra-creamy Greek yogurt and a lump of Cheddar that had been there for weeks. Evie grated the cheese over their potatoes while her dad grilled the sausages.

They sat and ate in silence, both busy with their own thoughts. George, Evie's dad, seemed particularly preoccupied this evening. It was quite normal for him to have a lot on his mind and Evie was used to him staring into space for long intervals while he pursued his own train of thought. She knew he often had problems at work, although quite what these problems were she wasn't sure. His job at a local computer firm meant he had to drive round the area 'installing systems', whatever that meant, and sorting out people's problems when those systems went wrong. 'Troubleshooting', he called it. Troubleshooting seemed to involve sitting on the phone for hours at a time telling the invisible person at the other end to 'click on this' or to 'delete that'. It would be nice if real life could be like that, Evie reflected, if you could just click on the bits you wanted to highlight, and delete the nasty bits. French homework, for example.

'Mum always liked sausages,' said George piling up their dirty plates. It was probably the only reference he would make to the anniversary, although the memory hung over them both like a black cloud. 'Are we eating dessert?'

They didn't usually, it was too much effort, but there was that Greek yogurt in the fridge.

'Something a bit naughty?' Evie suggested. 'There's bananas in the fruit bowl.'

'Why not? Go on.' He smiled at her.

'OK, you do the bananas and I'll do the rest.'

Together they concocted a mashed banana, brown sugar and yogurt extravaganza. There was no doubt that spontaneous puddings were always the best.

'Nice,' said George, as he swallowed his last mouthful. 'Although I think I prefer it with honey. So how was your day?'

'Mostly good,' said Evie. The yogurt on her spoon was streaked grey, a legacy of the rollerball leakage. 'Maths test was a farce, but no one got more than seven out of 20 so it didn't matter that I got a rubbish mark. Went to Halfway House after school. Adam was there.' She told him about the song competition.

'Sounds like fun,' said George 'Are you going to give it a go?'

She nodded. 'Adam said he'd write me a song.'

'Good old Adam,' said her dad. 'What would you do without him, hey?'

'And Tom turned up, too, after football.' Evie considered for a fleeting moment whether it was the right moment to mention Dave and their date on Saturday, but decided against it. Plenty of time for that between now and the weekend.

'Hallo? Anyone there?' George broke into her thoughts.

Evie sat up straight and mentally called herself to order. 'Sorry. Just thinking about all the homework I've got to do.' This was a well-tried scam she'd developed to get out of washing up.

'Of course. You go up and get on with it, I'll do the dishes.' Almost too easy. 'Oh, and Evie—'

'Mm?'

'OK if I go out for a bit later on? Said I might go and fix Julie's tumble dryer.'

'No probs.' He quite often went round to the Kendalls if there was something that needed mending or if Adam's mum had a paperwork crisis. He'd been doing it for years, long before his own wife died. 'It's no joke being left to cope with two small boys and no husband,' he used to say to Evie's mum, and she willingly loaned him out for the odd hour or two. Since Tom and Adam had grown up he wasn't needed so often, as the two boys were more than capable of helping their mum with things like cutting the grass and painting, but Julie still needed assistance with financial stuff. Troubleshooting, if you like. George's speciality.

***

Surprisingly, Adam was not at all happy about her going out with Dave.

'But, Evie, we always do things together on a Saturday night. I'd thought we could plan something for the singing competition.'

'Yes, but it's not as if we haven't got the rest of the weekend. It doesn't matter when you and I get together.'

'I've got other things going on. I'm supposed to be going to see my gran on Sunday. And a whole lot of coursework.'

'Ad, don't be so difficult.'

There was a pause. 'Do you really like this guy, Evie?'

'No, course not. Well, I don't know. Yes I do. Look, I've only just met him, for goodness' sake.'

'I don't think he's really your type.'

'What do you mean? Why not my type? What's wrong with him?'

'I can't explain. It's just something I feel.'

'You're talking drivel,' she said exasperatedly. 'If you want to know, I fancy him to bits, and if I want to go out with him, I will. It's not really anything to do with you anyway.'

'Yes it is. I'm your best friend. I've known you all my life and I just don't think you and Dave are suited.'

'But you got on so well with him. You really liked him.'

'I know. Call it a gut feeling, but I can't help thinking you and him together are a bad idea.'

'Adam, I really don't know what you're on about,' said Evie crossly. 'If you're peeved that I can't meet you on Saturday night, why don't you just say so? You've never had issues with any of my friends before.'

There was another pause. At last Adam said abruptly, 'OK, have it your own way. We'll make it Sunday afternoon for talking about the song. Late afternoon, then I can fit my gran in as well.'

He rang off and Evie sat at the kitchen table staring distractedly at the phone. It wasn't like Adam to be so moody about who she spent time with. It was almost as if he was jealous, as if he... But, no, that was a ridiculous idea. Not after all these years.

She shook herself and stood, stretching. Time for bed.

The door of the back bedroom opposite hers was wide open. The computer sat there invitingly, beckoning her to check her emails. She knew it would be cold in there - the radiator had been turned off to save energy - but perhaps she'd just have a quick look.

Vicki was already online.

hi evie
hi vick. orite?
yes good. u?
yes. v good
went well then did it?
wot went well?
u and brad pitt lookalike durrr. left u gazing in2 each
others eyes wen i went home didnt i?
and WOT eyes. sooooo cool going to party on sat with
him
no way!!!!!!!!! howju pull that?
natrl charm. adam not pleased tho
why not?
cant say. doesnt like him for sum reason
that's not like ad
i know

The screen was blank for a moment, then Vicki wrote:

hey eves, gess wot i found out about dave
wot
he does modelling!!! mostly on saturdays. adverts for
marshalls sportswear
howju no?
daniel rimmer told me, he sez its cos daves good at keep
ups
wots keep ups?
bouncing balls on yr knees
no way hosay. how duz bouncing balls advertise clothes?

i spose if you wear the kit and do something sporty it looks like its the kit gives you the skills. or something *keeeewerl!! shld i go to party? don't like ad being grumpy* course u shld. but wot about daves views on god?
do they matter?
adam mite think so
tuff. only a party, not lifetime comitmnt
kwite rite. not 2 be missed. fancy snogging those teeth
lol. innit.

The messages stopped for a couple of minutes and Evie thought Vicki must have gone. Then another line flashed up.

r u going on activity w/e in wales with gang from HH?
wen is it?
half term
yes, if dad lets me. if enuff money
me 2 shld be good
gtg. freezing in here
ok byeeeee
nite

Evie logged off the computer and watched as it closed down. The usual little box flashed up in the middle of the screen. *It is safe to turn your computer off now.* That's what she wanted; a special message from God telling her everything was fine. It is safe to go out with Dave Norfolk now.

There was no real reason to worry. Vicki seemed to think it was OK. If only Adam hadn't reacted the way he did.

No good talking to Dad: his troubleshooting didn't extend into the realm of boys and parties. Mum would've known what to do, but then Mum wasn't there any more.

***

By the next day there was already a new poster about the song contest pinned to the noticeboard in the entrance hall of Stanworth High. There was a buzz of chatter as large groups of people hung around the foyer, volunteering opinions on who should enter and who might win. Adam, always earlier to school than Evie, waylaid her as she walked through the big glass entrance doors. He waved a sheet of paper at her excitedly.

'I've got all the blurb here about the competition! It's amazing, Evie, the winner will get to be on telly!'

'How does that work?'

'It's a sort of talent spotting thing. Like *Pop Idol*. Only it's 'specially for people aged between 14 and 18. There are three rounds altogether and the person who wins the final gets to represent the town in a national competition next year.'

'Can anyone go in for it?' asked Evie, 'Don't you have to get through some sort of audition?'

'No, course not, that's the whole point of having three rounds. All you have to do is have a good song and be brave enough to stand in front of a panel of judges and sing it. Every entry has to be different. You can have live backing or use a tape, it doesn't matter which. We could do a tape for the first round, then I'd have time to write something special for the other two.'

'That's assuming we got through the first one,' said Evie, dubiously. 'Sounds a bit scary. Why hold it at Halfway House? Why not one of the school halls?'

'No idea. P'raps 'cause it's about the only place in town where kids from all the schools come together socially and it's kind of neutral territory. Though I don't s'pose they'll be able to keep Greenlands and Stannie High from falling out. But don't you think it sounds cool?'

'I guess so.' She was beginning to warm to the idea. 'So who are the judges?'

'That's the really amazing part,' said Adam. 'Barraclough! My piano teacher! And not just him, but one of the teachers from Greenlands as well. He's OK, Barraclough, I don't think he'll give us a hard time.'

'Yeah, but him knowing you personally is going to work against us, isn't it?' Evie pointed out. 'He's not going to want to look as if he's got favourites. 'Specially as he teaches you.'

Adam waved a hand airily. 'Oh, Barraclough's not like that. He'd be quite impartial. He teaches at other schools besides Stannie anyway. Besides, it's you who'll be singing and he doesn't know you. He might not even realise that it's me who's written your song.'

'If we ever get that far. Who are the other judges?'

'OK, listen to this, it'll blow your mind. One is Shelley who runs Shelley's Boutique in Market Street.'

'What, the stick insect?' Evie had often seen her hanging around at the back of the shop, a miniscule clothes horse with a huge personality. She looked as if she weighed about five stone and always wore outrageous make-up and unbelievably high heels. 'Well, I can see why she might be a good choice, I s'pose she'd have lots to say about style and image. And the other?'

'Vernon Eastwood from Thirty-Seven in Duke Street.'

Evie made a face. Thirty-Seven was where Dave was going to take her on Saturday. The place was well known among the clubbers of Stanworth. Not that she'd ever been there before, since a) you had to be over 18 and b) her father was convinced it was some kind of evil underground drugs den. Some of her school friends had been, though, either sneaking in unchecked, or using fake ID. Vernon Eastwood who owned the cellar bar was a notorious local figure, famous for his black eyepatch which was rumoured to conceal a glass eye, and even more so for the malicious humour which he used to great effect when ejecting undesirables from his cellar. The thought of him listening to her singing and passing judgement on it was terrifying, to say the least.

'Oh, Ad, I don't think I really want to do this.'

'Don't be such a ninny. He can't be that bad. He won't be any worse to you than anyone else. Anyway, I haven't told you the really big thing.'

'What's that, then?' Evie wasn't sure she wanted to hear any more.

'For the final round, right, the one where they pick the person who's going into the national televised thing, they've got Johnny Harker of Delusion.'

'You're winding me up.'

'No, really. Don't forget he comes from round here so he's got a big interest in the area. Even went to school at Greenlands.'

'So he'll be on their side, then.'

'Look, are you a big wuss or what?' said Adam with some exasperation. 'This is an opportunity you'll never get again and all you do is stand there wittering on about how useless you are. Stop stressing, will you?'

The pips were sounding for the first period of the day. Adam stuffed the piece of paper into his sports bag. 'I've got maths now. Probably won't see you again today 'cause our timetables are so different. But I'll be at Halfway House tonight and I'll bring some backing tapes. Just make sure you're there.'

'OK, Adam,' said Evie meekly. She could always argue with him later.

Three

Duke Street was a narrow road running parallel to Stanworth High Street. From the outside you would never have known Number Thirty-Seven was the coolest venue in town; the only indication that it existed was a small unobtrusive sign bearing the club's name in simple gold letters above a plain black-painted door. To the left of the entrance were three identical shuttered windows, which completely prevented anyone outside from looking in. During the daytime it had a slightly seedy air about it. Occasionally the unglamorous sound of a vacuum cleaner could even be heard wafting out into the street, but at night it seemed mysterious and exciting.

A large man in a tight waistcoat stood at the front, checking the ID of each person who went in. Evie, used to the welcoming open door of Halfway House, viewed this rather more sophisticated venue with awed respect.

'Are you sure we're allowed in here?' she whispered to Dave, as they approached the entrance.

He tapped the side of his nose. 'Trust me. I have the invitation. That's all we need.'

The card did indeed appear to have magic properties. In fact, the man at the door took one look at Dave and waved him through as though he'd known him for years. For a second he looked questioningly at Evie.

'No worries. She's with me,' said Dave. 'Where's the party?'

The man nodded and gestured to a long white-painted stone staircase behind him. 'Down there. Tropical Room.'

The party hit them like a blast as they entered. Intense heat, revolving coloured lights, pounding music, dozens of sweaty bodies. It was quite a big room but every inch was filled with people, dancing or standing in groups, trying to make themselves heard above the noise. Against one of the walls stood a huge glass tank full of exotic tropical fish. Hidden lights shone into the tank making its occupants look like vivid streaks of rainbow lightning as they darted about among the weed and stones at the bottom.

'Wow,' breathed Evie.

Dave grabbed her hand and pulled her over to the bar, brushing against several dancers as they went. Evie recognised a few of them as people who used to be at her school, all two or three years older than her. Several people greeted Dave. She guessed they must be friends from the Sixth Form College.

'Drink?'

A fleeting memory of all the bargains and promises she'd made her dad flashed through her mind.

'Um, OK, just a Coke.'

He bought her a Coke and a lager for himself and guided her over to a space where they could watch the action. People clustered together shouting and laughing, everybody seeming to know everybody else.

'Hey, look, isn't that thingamajig – you know, the guy who owns this place?' Evie exclaimed, suddenly catching sight of a familiar figure leaning against the bar.

'Vernon Eastwood. Yeah that's him.'

Vernon Eastwood it was, with stubbly greying hair, black silk shirt and legendary eyepatch. Exactly like he always looked in the pictures in the local paper.

'Is it true he has a glass eye under the patch?' yelled Evie over the noise of the music.

'Apparently,' shouted Dave. 'No one knows how he lost the eye. I've heard it said he got in a fight over someone's wife, but I don't know the details.'

'He looks mean.'

'Why, just 'cause of the eyepatch?'

'No, there's something about him...' But she couldn't put her finger on what it was.

'C'mon, let's dance.' He pulled her into the crowd of bodies on the dance floor.

Dave was an incredible dancer, far too good for Evie who could only manage a bog-standard bop. People stood back to watch as he gyrated round the floor, hips swivelling in time with the beat. John Travolta, eat your heart out, thought Evie. All he needs is the white suit. If only Vicki could see me now.

'Where did you learn to dance like that?' she asked later, as they downed well-earned drinks.

'Dunno. Picked it up as I went along. You learn a few things when you're advertising stuff.'

'That's all very well, but it shows the rest of us up,' she complained, scowling.

'Don't sulk,' he said, touching her nose with his forefinger. She stopped frowning and gave him a smile, suddenly shy. Her hair had gone damp from all the physical exertion and she could feel the wispy bits at the front taking on an annoying curl. She'd spent a whole hour with her hair straighteners before coming out. What a waste.

It had been a serious business getting this evening organised. First there'd been her dad to tackle. His initial reaction had been a straight 'no'. He'd heard what a den of iniquity the cellar was from other parents; as far as he was concerned she'd be forced to take in gallons of intravenous alcohol and there'd be free heroin given out at the door. Evie, expecting this response, set about the long slow business of softening him up. It wasn't like that at all, she told him, with totally ill-founded confidence. Mandy next door was allowed to go there quite regularly, and she wasn't a mainliner was she? They'd have to pay for every drink at club prices and she hadn't enough money to get even slightly tipsy. And she would be going with Dave who was a friend of Tom's, and probably Tom would be there too – good old Tom, who'd been a family friend since the world began.

'Is Adam going?' her dad had asked, but she'd waved the question aside and changed the subject. Eventually he'd given in, but not till he'd exacted all kinds of irritating promises about times of getting in and what she would drink and what she wouldn't smoke/swallow/inhale/inject. Evie could usually wear him down if she tried hard enough. She knew how much he hated arguments and she also knew he wanted her to have fun. It was a kind of ritual they always had to go through, this list of objections every time she wanted to do something new, but she could nearly always get him to say 'yes' in the end. In fact, it could be a bit disconcerting how easily she could make him give way.

Then there'd been the knotty problem of what to wear. She'd gone through her whole wardrobe trying stuff on and throwing it onto the floor in disgust. She was an OK shape generally, quite skinny really, and a fairly average height, so why did all her clothes make her feel so boring? And her face. Not pretty in the usual model girl sort of way, but all right if you like that sort of thing. At least she wasn't plagued with spots like some of the girls at school. Vicki always said she had a really nice crinkly smile and it was a pity it didn't appear more often. Evie felt this was a bit of a two-edged compliment: who wants a 'crinkly' smile? Crinkly sounded suspiciously like wrinkly. Anyway, the chief problem was that when she wore proper going-out type make-up she always felt like an ageing actress trying to cover her blemishes.

But here she was now, wearing Vicki's new silver top and black skirt – 'spill anything on it and I'll kill you' – with the fittest lad in the room, world probably, and he was looking at her as if he really fancied her. Could life be any better?

'Here's Fitz,' shouted Dave, as a shortish stocky youth in a purple shirt came over to them. Fitz was one of the three Sixth Form College boys whose party it was; Evie hadn't caught his real name properly in all the noise. Somebody Fitzpatrick or something like that, she thought Dave had said.

There was a lull in the music and for a moment you could hear yourself speak. 'Having a good time?' said Fitz. He looked at Evie with open interest and added to Dave. 'Is this her? The one you said—'

'Yeah, yeah, this is her,' said Dave, quickly. 'Great party. How did you get Vernon Eastwood to come in?'

'Oh, he always looks in at every event in his club. It's part of the deal. Likes to keep an eye on things. Mostly hangs out in the main room upstairs, strictly for the over-18s, but when there's a party like this he always shows his face for a bit. Prob'ly 'cause we're his future punters once we start earning proper dosh.' Looking at Evie again, he added, 'Dave met you in another club didn't he? That place halfway up the hill? How does it compare with this?'

'Oh it's *quite* different,' said Evie. 'It's just a sort of church youth club...' Suddenly Halfway House seemed very unexciting and juvenile compared with this noisy, colourful place.

Fitz's eyes glazed over. 'Sounds great,' he said politely. 'More drinks? My dad's given me some cash so I can buy stuff at the bar for my friends.' He disappeared into the crowd and emerged a few minutes later holding two tall glasses containing a clear liquid with ice and cherries floating on the surface.

'Try those, they should do the trick.' He gave a big wink to Dave, patted him on the arm and melted into the mass of heaving bodies.

'What does he mean, they should do the trick?' asked Evie.

Dave avoided her gaze. 'Just a figure of speech.'

'Yes, but why should they do the trick? What trick?'

He took a sip from his drink. 'It's just an expression. Look, I gotta go to the little boys' room. Are you OK for a minute? Go and look at the fish or something.'

He was gone for far more than a minute; in fact it was nearer ten. Evie actually saw him emerge from the Gents on the far side of the room but then he got caught up talking and laughing with a group of his friends. She stood all alone for a while trying to look moody and interesting so that no one would feel sorry for her and then began to wonder if she should she go and join him. Or would that look desperate?

A few moments ago everything had seemed so promising, but now she felt like a little girl being taken out for a treat who had become a bit of a nuisance. Suddenly she wanted to go home.

The glass in her hand was warm and sticky. She sniffed it gingerly. It didn't smell of anything much but she knew drinks could be deceptively strong. Who knew what might be in it? She'd promised her dad she'd stick to Coke. She looked around for somewhere to put it down but there were no surfaces near her and she was too tightly hemmed in by the crowd to get to a table without spilling it; she was stuck with it. Would Dave think she was a wuss if she didn't drink it? It was a big glass, and she'd no idea whether it was filled to the brim with spirits or was completely innocuous.

She peered into the tank on the wall beside her. A little yellow and black striped fish was gazing out at her, his small round mouth opening and shutting in an 'o' of surprise.

'Hallo, little fish,' she said, but her words were lost as the music started to belt out again.

Did fish get thirsty? It must be incredibly boring to never have anything but water to drink. She reached up and lifted the lid half an inch, resting her glass on the edge of the container.

'Fancy something a bit stronger?' For a moment the fish looked even more startled, then he flipped his tail and darted off to the other end of the tank.

Perhaps not, it might poison him. On the other side of the tank stood a large earthenware tub containing an exotic creeper that climbed along a trellis on the wall. She reached across and dumped the contents of her glass into the pot. The cherries sloshed around on the earth for a moment, and then made themselves little nests where they settled.

That was the end of *that*.

She looked up furtively, wondering if anyone had seen her and immediately saw Vernon Eastwood across the dance floor. He was looking straight at her with his one eye, a sardonic little half-smile on his lips.

To her great relief she saw that Dave was struggling his way through the crowd back to her side.

***

'So how did it go?' Vicki was on the phone next morning before Evie had even woken up.

'What time is it for goodness' sake?'

'Twenty past eleven. How was it? Do you like him? Is he as perfect as he looks? Was it *lurve*?'

Evie yawned and looked at her watch. It was indeed twenty past eleven. Her dad must have let her sleep in and left for church on his own. 'Don't be so silly. It was just a party.'

'Oh, Eves, don't be so annoying! Tell me *now*. What was Thirty-Seven like? You're so lucky to have a dad who'll let you go there, not like my mum and dad.'

'Yeah. Well, I s'pose it was pretty cool. You could hardly move for people and it was very hot... Oh, by the way, I lost the button off your skirt, it kept sagging so there was this great big gap under the top and I had to keep hoicking it up.'

'Very sexy. And did you get completely wasted?'

'You know I don't drink. I promised Dad. But the creeper did,' she said, suddenly remembering.

'The creeper? What on earth...?'

'Never mind. Oh, and guess what, Vick, Vernon Eastwood was there. At the party. He really does only have one eye, Dave said so. Looks just like in the *Stanworth Echo*.'

'Awesome.' Vicki sighed with deep satisfaction. 'And was there a whole lot of snogging goin' on?'

'A bit,' said Evie. In fact, rather too much for her liking. Dave had been all over her by the end of the evening. Funny how you could think someone was really gorgeous and yet still want to keep them at a bit of an arm's length. Still, all things considered, it had been a good evening once he'd stopped gabbing with his friends and turned his full attention back to her. And he'd said he wanted to see her again.

'So are you, like, an *item* now?'

'I don't really know. He didn't actually say so. But he does want to get together again. He said he might think about coming to Halfway House after school again. Maybe even to the activity weekend in Llanwellyn if it doesn't clash with one of his advertising gigs.'

'Excellent!'

'Yeah, I guess so.' Evie wasn't too sure. Somehow Dave seemed a bit too sophisticated for Halfway House with his designer jeans and all. Also there was the Adam thing. But perhaps that was just a one-off; probably Adam had just been having a bad day. She'd see him this afternoon anyway, and surely everything would be OK when she'd told him all about her evening.

She dressed quickly and went to the kitchen to look for juice. No doubt her dad would want to have a major debriefing session, full interrogation under bright lights, blood tests for illegal substances, the whole works. But he was already out and had left her a note. As she'd suspected, he had gone to church, and then he'd be over at the Kendall's again. Julie must be having a whole lot of trouble with her tumble dryer.

***

The first round of the singing competition took place the following Friday evening after school. Friday was always a busy night at Halfway House. There was no need to rush home from school when there was the whole weekend ahead for homework, and the mood tended to be relaxed and noisy. Word about the contest had spread quickly and today the club was jammed with young people, many of them not regulars, all agog to see who would get through the first heat. The audience poured in off the street and wedged themselves into every corner. Lots of them sat around the café-style tables, two to a chair in some places, and the rest crammed into the three big sofas, leaned against the walls or sprawled on the floor. Near the bar Ben had constructed a small platform so that everyone could see the singers.

The judges, two men and two women, were already in place when the club opened, sitting in a row behind a long table borrowed from the church hall for the occasion. Ben, Master of Ceremonies for the evening, sat between the two women in the middle.

'What an odd mixture they look,' said Evie to Adam. The two of them were perched side by side on a computer chair, both trying not to fall off.

'Yeah, you wouldn't have any trouble playing "Spot the Teacher".'

His own teacher, Mr Barraclough, was well known on the school music circuit. He gave some kind of music lessons at practically every school in the area; but even if he hadn't, the woolly jumper and baggy brown trousers would have marked him out instantly as a teacher. The other teacher, head of music at Greenlands, was also easily identifiable by the smart jacket and skirt and the large pad of official-looking A4 paper on the table in front of her.

'What do you think the paper's for?' whispered Evie, anxiously.

'Taking notes, obviously,' said Adam. He smirked. 'Get it? Music teacher? Taking notes?' But Evie was far too preoccupied even to attempt a smile.

'Just look at Shelley. She must be a size six! And look at all that jewellery!' The tiny owner of Shelley's Boutique was perched on a chair behind the table in deep conversation with Ben. Her brown hair, cut almost to her scalp, stuck out in all directions, its casual wispiness combining with a perfect bone structure to give her the air of a malnourished pixie.

And next to Shelley was Vernon Eastwood, eyepatch in place, in a black T-shirt and an extremely expensive-looking black jacket. No way you could mistake *him* for a teacher, thought Evie. She was doing her best not to look straight at him in case he recognised her from last Saturday, although she knew she couldn't avoid his scrutiny when she got up to sing. With any luck he hadn't really seen her properly at the party. Perhaps his good eye wasn't all that good, or maybe he would have forgotten her.

Ben introduced the panel and spoke briefly about the order of the evening. There were to be 15 entrants altogether for the first round; Evie's slot was somewhere near the end. She recognised the first entrant, he was from Year Nine in her school. He wore a pair of nicely pressed jeans and a hoodie and looked about ten years old.

'Hope his mummy doesn't mind him being out so late,' said one of the Greenlands lads, not very quietly. Some of the audience sniggered and the boy flushed. He handed his backing tape to Sue, who was operating the sound system, and started to sing his song in a breathless squeak.

'Has his voice broken yet?' whispered Adam to Evie.

'Ssh.'

When the boy had finished, he stood still, waiting for the verdict from the judges.

Shelley was first. She leaned forward and spoke in a sugary voice, as if to a toddler. 'Well done, dear, that was a very good attempt. I liked your song and you moved quite nicely. I think you need to do something about your clothes, though. A great performer should always catch the eye as soon as he comes on stage.'

The two music teachers spoke next. Both had something nice to say about his choice of song and the way he'd sung it, but neither seemed to be over-impressed. Then it was Vernon Eastwood's turn.

'How old are you?' he asked without preamble.

'Fourteen.'

'Well, you don't look it. Can I suggest you go away and come back when you're older? I don't think you're really ready for the big time yet.'

'Ooh, nasty,' muttered Adam.

'Yes, but true,' whispered Evie. None of this was doing any good for the butterflies in her stomach.

Other contestants followed. Some were good, some mediocre, some – as Vernon was only too quick to point out – frankly terrible. Vicki was in the first category. Although not every note hit the mark she more than made up for it with her dancing. Shelley raved about her, and even Vernon simply said, 'Not bad.'

Evie's name was called and she handed her tape to Sue at the sound desk. After much debate she and Adam had chosen something relatively easy for the first round, a song from a West End musical. It wasn't particularly ambitious, but gave her plenty of opportunity to show off her voice. She'd tied her hair up into bunches on either side of her face – 'an ironic hairstyle' Adam insisted on calling it – and wore a deep pink, strappy top with wide trousers.

She took her place on the platform and waited for the music to begin. Nothing happened.

'There's something wrong with this backing tape,' called Sue.

'Go and help her, would you, Adam,' said Ben, exasperatedly.

A long pause followed while Adam and Sue fiddled with knobs and experimented with speakers.

Someone started a slow handclap. Evie began to sweat. She stood on the platform clutching the microphone and looking round desperately. Her discomfort increased as she caught sight of Dave, lolling against the wall at the back and grinning at her; she hadn't known he was planning to come. Tom was with him, as usual.

She became aware that Vernon Eastwood was looking at her with some interest. Clearly he'd recognised her, and his dawning smile showed that he'd remembered where he'd last seen her. Flip.

The tape was working at last, so Evie pulled herself together and started to sing. All at once she felt recklessly confident. It couldn't be any worse than it'd been so far. She threw herself into the music and gave it all the feeling she could muster, finishing on a tremendous high note which she managed to hang on to far longer then ever before.

There was a short silence and then a noisy round of applause. She'd done OK.

'Yes, I really liked that,' said the music teacher from Greenlands.

'A strong musical performance,' said Mr Barraclough.

'Lovely hair, dear,' said Shelley.

Vernon Eastwood leaned back in his chair and sucked his pencil. 'Nice to see you again. Feel as though we're old friends.'

Evie blushed crimson. But he continued smoothly, 'Well, once the music started, it was a creditable effort. Well done.'

She left the stage, sank cross-legged onto the floor at Adam's feet and allowed herself to breathe freely.

'Quality stuff,' he whispered, bending to her level. 'Although I can't think what on earth he meant about you being old friends. Did you see Dave and Tom come in?'

She nodded. Suddenly she was exhausted, it had been a very long evening. There were only two more entries and a few people were beginning to slip out.

***

It was after nine when she got home, and she'd still had nothing to eat. Her dad was tinkering with the cistern on the bathroom toilet.

'How did it go? Did you get through the first round?'

'I did! Although it was nearly all ruined by the backing tape going wrong. But Ad managed to fix it in the end.

Shelley – you know, from the dress shop – she said I had lovely hair. What are you doing to the toilet? It's not broken, is it?'

'No, I just thought the cistern was taking too long to fill up. I wanted to get it timed properly. Pass me the screwdriver, would you?' He tightened a bolt then sat on the lid. 'So what was the competition like? Were you the best?'

'Certainly not the worst. There was this lad called Paul, though, right at the end; he was sensational. Don't think I can beat him. He was like every good singer you ever heard all rolled into one.'

'He can't have been that good.'

'He was. The judges thought so, too. Anyway, we're down to ten now and the next round is in a month.'

'And Vicki? Is she through as well?'

'Yep. Cool, isn't it? And Dave was there and he said afterwards I was awesome. Can you believe that? Awesome!'

George looked puzzled. 'Dave. Now which one is he? Is he one of your youth group?'

'Dad!' Evie threw up her hands in despair. 'You know. The boy I went to the party with last weekend. The one you made such a fuss about.'

Her dad's brow cleared. 'Oh yes. Adam's friend. I remember.'

'Not Adam's, Tom's. Tell you what, Dad, you stick to toilets and troubleshooting and I'll get on with my singing career. Is there anything to eat? I'm probably going to die of starvation if I don't consume at least five thousand calories in the next ten minutes.'

Singing loudly to herself she went to the kitchen and set about making one of her favourite triple-decker sandwiches: cheese, lettuce, bacon, cucumber and piles of mayonnaise squidging out at the bottom.

She was still in the competition and Dave thought she was awesome. Life was looking pretty good.

Four

The Halfway House trip to Wales took place a week later. Twenty-two members of the youth group had signed up to go, enough to fill two minibuses.

St Michael's only possessed one vehicle, an ancient white van with hard plastic seats and a strong smell of petrol. One or two of the seats had springs so close to the surface you could see their shape under the black plastic coating. The other minibus was borrowed for the weekend from Greenlands High. It was a recent donation to the school from the PTA, painted shiny bottle-green, the Greenlands colour, with the school crest on the side of the sliding door. The inside was roomy and comfortable, the seats were properly upholstered and the dashboard sported a state-of-the-art entertainment system. Not surprisingly, everyone wanted to travel in the Greenlands bus.

Evie was one of the lucky ones. It was a long journey, about three and a half hours in all, and made slower by Friday evening traffic; it seemed that the whole world had poured onto the roads for half-term. But she was able to travel in comfort at the end of a triple seat next to Vicki and Jade Abbot, a girl from her school, while Dave, Tom and Adam sat behind them. Evie had been really surprised that Tom had come along too; he'd been on these weekends before and had got very impatient with the Christian talks, but presumably Adam had persuaded him. As for Dave, the only reason she could think of for him being there was because she was. Scary thought. Surely it wasn't really just for the activities?

It was pitch dark by the time they turned into the drive of the Centre. As they pulled off the main road the bus headlights lit up a large sign by the gate bearing the words: 'Llanwellyn Christian Outdoor Pursuits Centre'.

'What's a Christian Outdoor Pursuit when it's at home? What makes it different from any other kind of outdoor pursuit? Do we have to sing hymns on a mountainside?' asked Dave. He was sitting next to the window directly behind Evie, and from time to time during the journey his hand had reached out in the darkness to squeeze hers.

Jade Abbott sniggered. 'Yeah, like Julie Andrews in *The Sound of Music*. The hills are alive...'

'That's not a hymn, eejit.'

'It's not the pursuits that are Christian, numbskull,' said Tom, 'it's the Centre.'

'Oh. Not very clear, is it?'

They came to the end of the long drive and drew up in front of a large country house. Two young men and a blonde-haired girl in red tracksuits were waiting at the door to welcome them. The house was definitely less grand on the inside than it appeared to be from outside: the walls were painted a shiny institutional cream and the floors were covered in hard-wearing coarse carpets. But there were still mouldings on the ceilings that must have been left from the days when it was a family home.

They were taken to their dormitories. The girls' rooms were at the top of the wide staircase, one on each side of the landing, and the boys' were in an annexe in the garden. Every dorm was equipped with bunk beds, one small wooden chest of drawers between two and a chair for each occupant. Evie found herself sharing with Vicki and Jade and four other girls. Tom, Dave and Adam were also in a dorm together.

It was quite late in the evening by the time they had all unpacked and regrouped for soup and sandwiches in the main lounge. Several of them had eaten chips at the service station on the way and no one was very hungry. The sitting area was full of rather shabby armchairs arranged in rows round the room. There was a television in the corner, a big fireplace containing a dried-flower arrangement and the walls were covered with several large paintings of local landscapes.

'Why's everyone so quiet?' said Vicki in an undertone to Evie as they sipped their soup in almost total silence. It was almost unheard of for the group to make so little noise.

Evie shrugged. 'Shy? Anyway, not everyone's quiet,' she added, nodding at Brooksie and Jade lurking by the door. 'What's up with them?'

'Need a fag, I should think,' grinned Adam. Brooksie and Jade were famous smoking buddies.

One of the young men who had greeted them at the door stood up in the middle of the room to address them. There was a logo on his tracksuit top, a white cross entwined with a roll of climbing rope, and underneath the letters LCOPC.

'Evening, everyone. Welcome to Llanwellyn. My name's Gareth and I'm one of the instructors here. You also met Heidi and Wayne as you came in: Heidi's from Switzerland, and Wayne is from Australia. He waved a hand at Heidi and Wayne who sat smiling behind him. 'And I'm from Wales – about one mile away, in fact.'

Tom gave a muffled snort and murmured 'Heidi! You have to be joking.'

'Cuck-oo,' trilled Dave under his breath.

'First, a few ground rules,' continued Gareth. 'One. Everyone has to help at mealtimes with washing up and setting the tables. I'll get Ben to divide you all into teams and each team will have one turn.'

There was general groan.

'Two. No boys in the girls' rooms at any time. Got that? Not at any time. And in case you're wondering, the same goes for girls in boys' rooms. Practically punishable by death.'

A few whistles and calls of 'Shame!' greeted this announcement.

'Three. You may not leave the grounds without permission. We need to know where you all are at any given moment. And four. Absolutely no cigarettes or alcohol allowed on the premises. OK? Any questions?'

There was some shuffling and muttering; for one moment it looked as though Brooksie was going to object to the cigarette rule, but Jade was nudging him to be quiet and giving him meaningful looks. 'Can't see them sticking to *that* one,' whispered Vicki to Evie.

'We have a full programme tomorrow. Breakfast at eight, then morning on the assault course or high ropes. Sandwich lunch, and in the afternoon a choice of hillwalking, abseiling or canoeing. Time to yourself for an hour at five, evening meal at six, gathering here for a short talk from Ben at seven-thirty, bed at ten. Perhaps a bit of in-house entertainment before bed. How does that sound?'

'Ex-haus-ting,' said Jade with feeling.

'Physical activity not really your thing?' asked Dave. He looked at her with interest. Jade was having a blue month: she liked to change her hair colour on a regular basis. Not all of it, just the top of her head, leaving the ends black. Last month it had been green, the month before an astonishing shade of orange.

'Totally not.'

'So why are you here?' But Jade just smiled noncommittally, revealing a shiny silver stud on her tongue.

'For the fellas, if I know Jade,' whispered Evie to Vicki, then felt a bit guilty.

***

Saturday morning was clear and bright; the sort of morning when you felt there really was a hope winter might soon go away for good. It was bit too early for daffodils to bloom in their full splendour, but here and there they were beginning to open in little clumps. In daylight the view from the girls' dorm was truly spectacular, looking out onto the large sports field behind the Centre and a range of craggy heather-covered hills beyond.

They had lain awake talking far too late the night before. It had been nearly three o'clock in the morning when the last of them had finally fallen asleep. Jade had been the chief culprit; each time they had been about to drop off she had thought of some other riveting topic to discuss, mostly to do with the boys in the group. Evie was seriously beginning to wonder if she could stand a second night in the same room.

Just before she'd fallen asleep her mobile had beeped with a text from Dave. *Sleep well xxx* said the words on the little screen, shining like a beacon in the darkness.

'What are you doing today?' Adam asked her, standing in the breakfast queue in the large sunny dining room. He looked slightly the worse for wear, as if the boys' dorm had also been up half the night talking.

'Hum. Not sure. Maybe the assault course in the morning. Thought I might do the hillwalking after lunch. What about you?'

'High ropes, I think. And then hillwalking. Tom and Dave as well.'

'Cool. I think Vicki probably will too. So you and Dave are big mates now.'

'Course we are. We never weren't. Don't know where you got that idea from.'

'Could it have been something to do with the fact that you practically refused to speak to me when I wanted to go out with him?'

'Yeah, well, I still don't think it's a great idea.'

'Really? Shame. That's not what Dave thinks,' grinned Evie, piling Shreddies into her bowl.

It was a bit strange being away for the weekend with someone you really fancied. She couldn't quite bring herself to call him her boyfriend yet, as so far she'd only been to the one party with him, but he always seemed to be wanting to sit next to her or giving her extra smiles when she looked his way. An activity centre wasn't really conducive to blossoming passion, she decided, munching her stringy bacon and tinned tomatoes. Everything was much too highly organised. If you were looking for a romantic atmosphere you'd be sadly disappointed.

She quite enjoyed the morning on the assault course, organised and led by Heidi. The instructor turned out to be frighteningly athletic. Nothing was beyond her. First she demonstrated the course at enormous speed, then with the aid of a whistle and a thunderously loud voice she cajoled her group up a sheer wall, across a stomach-lurching wooden bridge, through a claustrophobically narrow tunnel, over the river on a rope and from one end of the death slide to the other. Even the boys were impressed at their own skill. Evie, not the bravest of individuals, could hardly believe that she'd managed to finish it. You couldn't help feeling quite pleased with yourself after completing such a demanding course. If you could do all that you'd be ready to have a go at anything.

By comparison the hill walk looked much easier. There were ten of them tackling it, led by Wayne. They were taken to the starting place in the minibus, about twenty minutes' drive from the Centre, and deposited in the car park with two maps, some chocolate biscuits and several bottles of water. They could see the stony path winding up the hill beyond a gate; it was quite wide and well defined with only a gentle incline. Sheep grazed peacefully on either side of the track.

'Complete doddle,' said Dave, looking up the hill. 'Be up and down in five minutes.'

'Don't you believe it,' said Wayne. 'It gets a lot steeper higher up and the path becomes less clear. Also the weather can change very suddenly without warning.'

'Yeah, yeah.'

They began to climb, in a single group at first, then dividing into little groups of two or three. Almost at once Evie found herself walking beside Dave, speeding up her step to keep pace with his long-legged stride.

''S'nice here,' he said looking round appreciatively at the wild daffodil buds and the distant range of hills. Fluffy white clouds scurried across the sky and a large unidentifiable bird soared above them.

She nodded. 'Beats Stanworth.'

'Mind you, those beds take some explaining. Talk about creak. Tom was on the one above me, and every time he turned over I thought we were being invaded by aliens. How you're supposed to sleep with that noise going on over you. In the end I took my mattress off and slept on the floor by the door. Only then there was a dreadful draught by my head. Not a good night.' He looked sideways at Evie. 'Did you get my text? You didn't reply.'

'Couldn't think of anything to say. But thanks, anyway.'

'Wasn't sure if you'd be asleep.'

'No one goes to sleep early on the first night. Probably will tonight though, we'll all be so knackered.'

'Have you been on one of these before, then?'

'Yes, about two years ago. Didn't come last year because of my mum.'

There was a silence. Dave, visibly uncomfortable with the subject, said awkwardly, 'Is it bad? Without your mum, I mean? Do you, like, miss her all the time?'

'No, not all the time. There are moments. For instance, when I want to tell her something. Or Mother's Day when everyone else has their mum. Or when I go back at the end of a weekend like this and Dad doesn't know the right questions to ask.'

'How do you manage? When you're feeling really bad, I mean.'

She considered. 'I guess the gang at Halfway House have helped a lot. Ben's great, and Sue. And friends like Vicki and Adam.'

'They're all Christians aren't they?'

'Yeah, I suppose they are.' She hadn't really made the connection. To her they were just her best friends.

'Does being a Christian help?' he persisted, as if he genuinely wanted to know. 'Do you think your mum's in heaven?'

'Yes, but not heaven with clouds and harps and stuff,' she said. She'd thought a lot about this. 'I just know she's happy with God. She always believed in him when she was on earth and she loved him a whole lot, and I have this really strong feeling that that still has to be going on. Only even better now she can actually see him.'

'Must be great to have beliefs like that,' said Dave, kicking a large lump of sheep-dropping out of his path. 'Something to lean on when things go wrong.'

'No, you don't understand, being a Christian isn't about being propped up. It's much more than that. It's more a case of seeing a reason for things and knowing there's someone who sees the bigger picture when you can't see why things are so horrible.'

'You mean, your mother dying was for a reason?'

'Yes. No. I don't know.' This wasn't going well. She'd wanted to tell him about what she believed but it had come out all wrong. Yet, funnily enough, it didn't alter the sure feeling she had about God, even if she couldn't express this trust in a way that Dave could understand. She thought about the cards and Bible verses friends had sent her when her mother died; concrete expressions of love. No one could take away what that had meant to her.

They were walking more slowly now, right at the back of the group. Dave reached out his hand and took hers. 'And what about Adam? Haven't you and he ever got it together? You're such good mates.'

Evie laughed. 'No chance. He's like a brother. The whole idea is totally gross.' The idea of her and Adam being anything but best friends was absurd.

Or was it? She knew she felt nothing like that for Adam, but supposing, just supposing, that was why he was so against her and Dave...

They tramped on in silence and then Dave pulled her hand and said, 'Let the others go on a bit. Let's stop and have our chocolate biscuits.'

They sat side by side on the damp grass and leaned against a rock. Dave's arm crept round her shoulder and the next few moments passed very pleasantly. After a bit he stroked her hair from her eyes and murmured, 'I'm glad I came. I nearly didn't, you know. It was only 'cause Tom decided to.'

Evie didn't reply. Her arms and legs seemed to have melted and she could actually hear her heartbeat.

'Are you glad I came?' he persisted.

She nodded, suddenly self-conscious, and looked away from him and up the hill. 'Shouldn't we catch up with the others? We've been here at least 15 minutes. It's getting really parky.' A wind was rising and it was beginning to feel extremely cold sitting on the wet ground. The little white clouds that had been scudding across the sky all afternoon were starting to look bigger and darker.

She stood, a little unsteadily, and reached out to pull Dave to his feet. He got up and nuzzled her neck above the collar of her fleece. She gave him a little push.

'Come on, Mr Sporting He-man. We're gonna have to get our skates on if we're going to catch up with them.'

They continued up the hill at a brisk pace through a long wooded area. The path was eerily silent and they climbed even faster, all the time expecting to see the others ahead of them.

'No worries,' said Dave, 'we'll see them as soon as we're out of the trees. We can't be that far behind. If Jade had been going any slower she'd have stopped.'

'That's the fags for you. Makes you seriously unfit,' said Evie, trying hard not to pant as she scrambled up the path behind him.

The track emerged from the trees and now they had a reasonable view ahead for some distance but there was still no sign of the rest of their party.

'You'd think they'd have waited for us,' said Evie, beginning to feel slightly annoyed.

Dave was looking at the sky. 'I don't like the look of those clouds. They're getting closer and closer. What's the matter with your friends, why couldn't they make sure we were still with them?'

'We did rather lag behind,' pointed out Evie irritably. His reference to 'your friends' had not passed unnoticed.

'OK, but Wayne is supposed to be looking out for all of us.'

'True. But you walk so fast it probably wouldn't occur to him that you might get left behind.'

Within a few minutes they were in thick cloud and could only see the path for a couple of feet in front of them. The air was cold and clammy, and little gusts of wind chilled them to the bone.

'Perhaps we should turn back,' suggested Evie.

'Then they'll never find us. They could be out here for ages searching for us.'

'Well, what do you suggest then, clever clogs?' They stood and stared at each other.

Without warning and apparently from nowhere the Indiana Jones theme tune filled the foggy air.

'Of course!' exclaimed Dave. 'Your mobile! Why on earth didn't I think of it?' Evie rummaged in her pocket to answer.

'Evie?' It was Adam. 'Where are you?' He sounded very cross.

'We're just a bit behind you. If you come back down the path you'll find us.'

'We *have* gone back down the path, miles and miles. We've been looking for you for ages.'

'You can't have. We're here waiting for you.'

There was a pause while Adam conferred with someone. Then a voice with a strong Australian accent took over. 'Evie? This is Wayne. Is Dave with you?

'Yes.'

'I think you must have missed a turning somewhere and got onto the wrong track. Can you see any obvious landmarks around you?'

'No, nothing. It's all mist.'

'OK, well, don't panic, we'll get you down. Probably the best thing is to turn round and come down the way you went. Do you think you can manage that?'

'I s'pose so. It can't be that difficult.'

'What did you say? I can't hear you very well?'

'I said that can't be difficult!' she shouted but there was no reply. Her phone emitted a faint beep. 'Oh no, can you believe it? My battery's going. I didn't bring my charger. We'll have to use your phone.'

'No good,' said Dave, 'I left it in the dorm. Thought there'd be enough other people with mobiles.'

She slipped the phone back into her pocket, suddenly aware of how alone they were. 'Well, Wayne says we have to go back the way we came.'

'OK, fine,' said Dave. 'I'll go first.'

But they had walked only a short distance when it became apparent that the path was becoming narrower and narrower until eventually it was just a sheep track plunging off into a forest of dead bracken. Undeterred, they followed it down, although the hillside was becoming gradually steeper and muddier and the track getting more and more difficult to see. At last the path petered out altogether.

'Now what do we do?' asked Evie. The mist was as thick as ever and she was beginning to feel moderately scared.

'Just keep going, I suppose,' said Dave. He didn't sound very confident.

They slithered downhill as best they could, partly upright and partly on their bottoms, sometimes catching hold of branches and bushes as they went. Evie's hands were a mass of blisters where she had caught at bracken stalks to steady herself. In some places the way down became so impassable that they had to climb up for a while until they could find another route.

Suddenly Evie tripped over a root. A stabbing pain shot though her ankle as her foot twisted back on itself. And she let out a bloodcurdling yelp.

At the same moment Dave exclaimed, 'Listen! Water!'

To their left a wide stream bubbled down the hillside. It was quite shallow; the water was very clear and full of pebbles and small rocks.

'That must be the stream that comes out by the car park!' he said. 'If we walk straight down there we'll be home and dry.'

'Hardly dry,' Evie wanted to say, but the pain from her ankle was so great that all she could manage was a whimper.

'Are you all right? Have you done something really bad?' Trying desperately not to cry she pointed at her foot. He knelt by her side and rolled back her sock to inspect the damage.

'I've got to get the boot off,' she said, starting to untie the laces. But he stopped her.

'No don't do that, it'll swell up and then you won't be able to walk at all. Look, you're going to have to put up with it just till we get down. Do you think you can do that?'

'No.'

'Evie, come on, don't be a wuss. It can't be far now. I'll help you.' He wrapped her arm round his neck and put his round her waist, helping her to her feet.

'Ouch!'

'OK, no hurry, we can do this. Just hang on to me.' Slowly, gingerly, he eased her towards the stream. 'How're you doing? Think you could manage to walk down through the water?'

'But it'll get into my boots!'

'It may do. But it's the only way.'

Very, very slowly they started to edge their way down the stream. The journey seemed to take forever. Evie could feel the icy water through her boots even though only a few drops actually seeped over the top. Once her socks were wet she lost all sensation in her toes from the cold. Her arm was hurting too, hooked round Dave's neck, and every time they went over a bump it felt as if it was being wrenched from its socket. Her hair was drenched from the mist droplets and a steady trickle of water dripped off her nose onto her chin.

It began to feel as if her whole life had consisted of this one journey down the stream through thick cloud, each step over the stones painfully slow, occasionally slipping on a slimy rock, the pain in her ankle constant. Every so often they paused to call to the others, then stood silently, straining their ears for a reply, hearing nothing but the sound of the stream gurgling over the rocks.

And then, magically, a shout.

'Evie! Dave! Can you see us? We're just down to your right. After the boulder!'

Beyond the big rock they glimpsed an unmistakeable blue flash of Jade's hair. Possibly the best sight in the world.

***

Apparently Evie's ankle was sprained, not broken. 'But you know, this can be just as painful as breaking,' said Heidi, in heavily accented English, as she strapped it up for her. 'If it is still big like this in the morning we must have an X-ray, but I am thinking it is just pulled ligaments.'

Heidi was a highly qualified First Aider. There seemed to be nothing she couldn't do.

Adam was less sympathetic. 'What on earth were you doing, wandering off like that?' he asked as he and Evie sat sipping hot chocolate in the communal lounge in the free half-hour before Ben's evening talk. She had had a reviving bath and the warmth of the drink seeped into her body filling her with a delightful sleepiness.

Jade, a few feet away, let out a smutty cackle. 'What do you think they were doing? Use yer noodle!'

Adam saw the blush creeping over Evie's face. 'Honestly, Eves, you can be such a *wally*.' He shrugged his shoulders, turned away from her and started talking to Brooksie on his other side. He seemed really cross, far angrier than the situation merited.

Why does my relationship with Dave upset him so much? wondered Evie once again.

Ben was calling for quiet. He opened his Bible and began speaking. His talk was about choices and the need for Christians to be willing to stand out and be different from everyone else. 'Do not be conformed to the world,' was how the Bible put it. There were lots of moments when you had opportunities to make decisions about how to act, but if you believed in God you would want to do what he wanted.

'It's easy to get distracted by feelings,' Ben went on, 'feelings can be incredibly strong, and sometimes they seem like they're the only thing that matter. If you let them be the thing that guides you, you can find yourself wandering into all kinds of trouble. A bit like Evie and Dave today,' he added, grinning. 'They thought they could find their own way, but look what happened to them.'

'Yeah, you go, Davie boy!' murmured someone and several people chuckled.

'Sometimes we have to make a deliberate choice to keep to the right path, and it isn't easy. But it is a choice; we don't have to follow the way of the world or our own feelings. Christians have the option of being different from everyone else. That's real freedom.'

'Yes, but how can that really be freedom?' interrupted Adam, suddenly sitting up straight and talking very quickly. 'If you're always doing what God wants, surely that only gives you one way to act in any situation. So, in fact, your freedom has gone.'

'Yeah, isn't freedom being able to do whatever you like?' said Brooksie, fingering the fags in his pocket. He was clearly finding the weekend a bit restrictive.

'Think about Evie and Dave on the walk,' said Ben. 'They were absolutely free to go where they wanted and that's what they did. But they found their choice created new problems and then they had to make more choices and so they got deeper and deeper into trouble. Their whole walk was one big effort to correct their original mistake. If they'd kept to the right path with Wayne they'd have been able to saunter along, joining in the banter, enjoying the view—'

'Yeah, right! Some view!'

'—completely confident in the knowledge that they were with an expert who knew the way,' continued Ben. 'That's how it works in our relationship with God. The next bit of the Bible talks about having our minds transformed. That means letting him become so much a part of us that we will know what he wants and what is best for us. So that we're walking with the expert, if you like. Then we can relax and enjoy the view along the way in complete freedom.'

Evie caught Dave's eye across the room. He was looking her intently, apparently watching to see her reaction. She suddenly felt overwhelmingly tired. It had been a very long day indeed.

Five

The swelling in Evie's foot hadn't subsided in the morning so to be on the safe side Heidi decided to take her to the local Casualty department. The X-ray showed that Heidi's diagnosis had been right: there was no break, but it would be some time before Evie would be able to walk comfortably again. The hospital supplied her with a pair of crutches and told her to rest the ankle as much as possible. The trip to Casualty had taken so long that she missed the whole of the Sunday morning at Llanwellyn.

'What a waste of a weekend,' she lamented to Vicki as they travelled home on Sunday afternoon. They were in the church minibus this time, and the other half of the group was having their turn in the posh Greenlands bus. Evie's foot still hurt when she put it on the floor so it was now propped up on the seat in front of her. It was slightly more comfortable that way, but it didn't stop the little arrows of pain that shot through her ankle every time they went over a bump.

'Well, at least Dave came,' said Vicki. Dave was at the rear of the bus with Adam and Tom, well out of earshot. The three lads were engrossed in a deep conversation and from time to time there were great shouts of laughter from the back seat.

'Fat lot of good that turned out to be,' Evie grimaced.

'Still, you'd never have got down the hill without him, would you?'

'Yeah, but I'd never have got lost in the first place without him, would I?'

'Takes two to tango,' put in Jade from the adjoining seat. 'I bet he didn't have to *force* you to go off with him.'

'We don't all have evil minds like yours, Jade,' said Vicki. Jade's activities with a whole succession of boys were the subject of regular gossip at Halfway House.

But Evie was preoccupied with a new thought. 'How'm I going to manage at the singing contest? I can hardly stand up there on crutches.'

'Mm. Tricky. You could give yourself a whole new image, perhaps. Evie Wilson, Stanworth's only one-legged songster.'

'It'd get you the sympathy vote,' said Jade.

'The one-eyed judge and the one-legged competitor. A special kind of fellow feeling,' said Vicki, warming to the idea.

Ben, at the wheel of the minibus, was eavesdropping on their conversation. 'Sorry to disappoint you, girls, but I think she'll be pretty well recovered by the next round of the competition. These sprains don't take long to mend. Do you want me to drop you off at your house, Evie, so you don't have to hobble home with your rucksack?'

Already they were driving through the suburbs of Stanworth only a few minutes away from the Wilsons' bungalow.

'Shame he can't drop us all home,' said Vicki, idly drawing stick men in the condensation on the minibus window. Suddenly she stopped, sat bolt upright, gave Evie a sharp poke in the ribs and pointed at the pavement outside.

'Oh... My... Word.'

'What?' Evie leaned over Vicki, completely obscuring her line of vision, and peered out.

A couple were walking along the pavement hand in hand. They had their backs to the bus and sauntered along in the sunshine, unaware of their audience and completely engrossed in each other. At one point the man leaned over and gave the woman a quick kiss.

It took several seconds for the realisation to dawn on Evie that the man was her own father. She stared out of the window in complete stupefaction.

'Who is it with him?' said Vicki.

Evie craned her neck for a good view of the woman's face as they drove past. There was a moment's silence as she tried to take in what she saw.

'Well?'

'It's Julie,' she said in a shocked voice, 'Adam's mum. Tom and Adam's mum. Wrapped round my dad.'

Vicki shot a fleeting glance to the rear of the bus. The boys on the back seat were completely oblivious to anything beyond their own conversation.

'Don't say anything to them,' said Evie quickly, signing to Vicki to keep her voice down so that Ben wouldn't hear either. She was going to need time to think about this on her own.

'Perhaps it's just a friend thing,' suggested Vicki, not very convincingly. 'They've been friends for years, haven't they?'

'Did it *look* like a friend thing to you?' said Evie.

Vicki had to agree that it didn't. 'Well, hey, it's pretty cool really, isn't it? I mean with you and Adam being such mates and everything. Perhaps you'll end up having him as a real brother.'

'Maybe it's been going on for a long time, ' said Jade, perking up. 'Like ages and ages. Two or three years or something and you never guessed. Just how romantic would that be?'

Evie shot her a crushing look. Her mother had still been alive two years ago so it certainly couldn't have been going on then... A sudden chill crept into the pit of her stomach.

All those evenings mending fences, fixing broken washing machines and helping with bills and tax returns. Had the whole thing been a front for something else? Could her father have had something going with Julie even then, even when her own mother was dying? In amongst all those hospital visits and the hushed voices and the calls from the Macmillan nurse?

Had her father been having an affair all the time?

Stupid, stupid idea. As if.

***

Things were going very well between Evie and Dave. After the weekend away he spoke to her nearly every day, either by email or by text messages and actual phone-calls. Occasionally he dropped by at Halfway House after school but he didn't usually stay very long, frequently going on to Tom and Adam's house. A couple of times he met her in town after school and they mooched around the shops together. Her ankle was making a good recovery and the crutches became unnecessary after a few days.

Adam was in the club less often in the second half of term. He told Evie this was because he had so much homework to do. He was having real problems putting her song together for the next round of the competition: although he had plenty of ideas about the kind of music he wanted to write, none of it suited her voice very well. The date for the next heat was approaching fast and he still hadn't managed to come up with anything. It seemed that they were both so busy they only ever saw each other at school.

'It hasn't got to be anything like the first song,' she told him, pausing briefly to talk by the lockers between lessons. 'In fact it'd be better if it was completely different. Something a bit more funky and cool.'

'Yeah, but your voice is more suited to ballady-type songs,' he said. 'It's no good me writing something hip hop or garage when really your strength is the Celine Dion-type big sound. Not that I could do hip hop even if I tried.'

'Dave thinks I should do a bluesy sort of song,' said Evie.

'Dave does, does he? What does Dave know about it, anyway?'

'Keep yer hair on. It was just something he said in an email last night.'

'OK, chill, I'm working on it. Are you going to see him again on Saturday or do you want to spend some time trying things out?'

Evie pondered. She had nothing definite fixed with Dave but she wanted to keep Saturday night free, just in case. On the other hand, she and Adam had got to get this song sorted or she'd end up at the second round with nothing to perform at all.

At length she said, 'Saturday's cool. See you then.'

***

But when she saw Adam on Thursday morning he looked white as a sheet and complained of a terrible sore throat. By Friday he was off school with flu.

His mum rang Evie to break the news. 'Really sorry, love, but I fear he's going to be in bed for several days. His throat looks as though it's been scraped with a cheese-grater and his temperature's going up and down like a yo-yo. No chance of him coming round to yours tomorrow night.'

Evie's heart sank. 'Did he say anything about the song?'

'No. Hang on, I'll ask him.' There was a muffled conversation in the background. Eventually Julie came back on the line. 'He says can you sort something out yourself? He doesn't want to leave it any nearer the time. He thinks Ben might be able to help.'

'No worries. Tell him to get better soon.' Evie rang off and stared dejectedly at a small puddle of milk on the kitchen table. She would have to use another backing tape for the second round, just when she'd been hoping that Adam would come up with something really original.

Later in the evening she logged on to the Internet to look for inspiration. Almost immediately a message from Vicki popped up in the bottom right-hand corner.

yo, dude
yo 2 u 2
hows trix?
bad. adam on his deathbed. no song for round 2 next week
baaadd. plan B?
havnt got one. only got as far as plan A
bummer
any ideas?
you can get good backing tapes on web. www.musicbackingtrack or something like that
not enuff time
or bens got CDs. quite good ones. he got mine
spose ill have to try that. wot r u doing for your song?
ahaaaaa. state secret. i could tell you but then i would have to kill you
thanx for sharing
hows the lovelife?

could be worse. yours?
dont change the subject. do u reely reely like him?
guess so
duz he want to sleep with u?
VICKIII!!!!!!
well does he?
dont know

Evie sat and thought for a moment, then she typed:

anyway im a christian. so r u so u shldnt have to ask
jenny b is a christian and she sleeps with her boyfriend
yeah well im not jenny b
wot if he threatens to dump u if u wont?
going now. byee

Evie logged off and sat chewing her nails. What if, indeed. She had a pretty strong feeling from things he'd said and the way he behaved that Dave wasn't going to be happy with just a kiss and a cuddle for much longer. It would be the first time her faith would have been put to this sort of test and she wasn't a hundred per cent sure she knew what she would do. She really did like Dave an awful lot and when his arms were round her and he was looking into her eyes she felt it would be perfectly normal and natural to carry their physical relationship further if that was what he wanted. But then there was this little voice which kept saying no, this was something to be kept for that one special person who she would be with for life. A little voice which she knew belonged to God. Although who was to say that Dave wasn't that one special person? Her dad had met her mum while they were still at school; why couldn't it happen to her too? And if so, what difference would a ring and a piece of paper make?

What was it Ben had said that time at Llanwellyn? Do not conform to the world. But wasn't there a danger you could become conformed to the *Christian* world, just because you'd never really thought it out for yourself, and you were scared of living? Most people at school thought Christians were repressed and prudish. Perhaps they were right. The Bible was written hundreds of years ago, so how could you work out what were meant to be rules for those days, and what teaching was meant to be followed for all time, today included? It was very puzzling.

Vicki wasn't much help. She asked all the same kind of questions as Evie was asking, but was totally hopeless at supplying any kind of answer. You would think, thought Evie as she started to get ready for bed, that a proper friend would be better at giving advice. It would make life a lot simpler if Vicki started leaping forward with lots of relevant Bible verses or direct messages from God.

In fact, come to think of it, where did it actually say in the Bible, 'Thou shalt not sleep with thy boyfriend'? There was all that stuff about not committing adultery, certainly, but wasn't that about when you were already actually married? Evie could see the point of having to stick with one person once you'd made the commitment; it was obvious there'd be all kinds of problems if you started fancying someone else. But who would it hurt if you simply wanted to show someone you really liked them and no one else was involved? There was such a very big gap between what she'd been taught at church and what her friends at school were doing.

Normally, she might have discussed it with her dad. Obviously not the nitty-gritty of whether she should sleep with Dave in particular, but the general principle of what was right and wrong. But right now even her dad no longer seemed the safe reliable fount of all knowledge he'd always been.

She would have to work this one out on her own.

Six

The second round of the competition drew an even bigger crowd than the first, the majority coming from Stanworth High and Greenlands. To make more space all the café tables had been stacked near the rear entrance so that the whole of the main club room could be used to accommodate the audience. There was a dire shortage of chairs, but four rows had been set out and after that it was a case of finding a gap on the floor. The bar was jammed full of provisions. Ben had ordered in extra supplies of fizzy drinks, chocolate and crisps, and besides all this he'd managed to beg several free grocery boxes of overripe fruit from Quikmart to make smoothies. Ben's eldest son, Noah was there to help serve drinks, and Sue was operating the sound system.

Evie arrived to find Tom and Dave waiting for her at the door.

'Did Adam come?' she asked immediately.

'Yeah, he's in there. Looking all pale and interesting.' Tom nodded at the back row of chairs where Adam had installed himself. He was indeed very white and had clearly lost some weight during his illness. There were dark shadows under his eyes and his naturally lean frame looked positively skinny.

Evie, looking round for Vicki, spied her squatting on the floor among a group of Greenlands Year Tens. She was wearing a white dress and had a new haircut. Evie waved at her and went to find herself a seat next to Adam, with Tom and Dave following close behind.

Evie was very nervous about the song she'd chosen for this round. It had turned out that Ben had quite a good collection of backing tracks and after a certain amount of dithering she'd settled for a Dizzie Diamond song. She really liked it but it was very different from the number she'd done in the first round. It also involved a lot more onstage movement, something she felt exceedingly self-conscious about and which had required several hours closeted in her bedroom in front of the long mirror.

Ben banged on the table and called for silence.

'Good evening, everyone. Welcome to Round Two of the Stanworth Music competition. And a special welcome to our judges and to those competitors who've made it into this heat.'

There were ten competitors left. Now that the obvious non-starters had all been removed the competition seemed to be hotting up, and the first three contenders drew a certain amount of grudging admiration from Shelley and the music teachers. However, Vernon Eastwood was a different proposition altogether. As far as he was concerned none of them was any good. Their clothes were uncool, they had picked the wrong songs for their voices, they couldn't sing in tune, and they moved like lumps of wood.

The fourth competitor was a rather tubby girl who went to the convent school just outside Stanworth. First it was her clothes that came in for Vernon's criticism.

'What size trousers do you take, my love?' he asked in deceptively honeyed tones.

The unfortunate girl coloured. 'It varies.'

'Wear a bigger pair, next time, will you? It looks to me as if the seams on those are working overtime.'

There was some unkind laughter and the girl blushed an even deeper red. Evie cringed in discomfort.

'And your song – "I will survive",' he went on. 'One of the great songs of our time, but only suitable for the strongest voice. Whatever made you choose it?'

She stared back at him silently.

'For a start you don't seem to have learned all the words, and even if you had, you haven't enough breath control to get them out clearly. It's a song to be sung with great passion. You have about as much passion as a damp dishcloth.'

'The rat,' muttered Evie.

'Delusions of grandeur,' whispered Adam. 'Thinks he's Stanworth's answer to Simon Cowell.'

Vernon was warming to his theme. 'Your first song was quite good, if I remember rightly, but this time you've bitten off more than you can chew. I'm afraid, my dear, you *won't* survive.' He scribbled something down on the pad in front of him and waved her off.

Next was Paul, the Greenlands boy who'd done so well in the first round. As soon as he opened his mouth Evie knew he was into the finals. Not only did he look the part, but he also had a genuinely impressive voice. Even Vernon grudgingly admitted his obvious talent.

One by one the competitors performed, some with a measure of confidence, others less so, until eventually only Vicki and Evie were left. One of the pitfalls of having a surname beginning with W meant that you were always at the end in everything. Vicki Stilwell, Evie Wilson.

Vicki's name was called. She handed her backing tape to Sue, moved onto the platform and waited for the music to start.

The moment she heard the opening bars Evie tensed in her seat. There was something extraordinarily familiar about the first few guitar chords. Where had she heard them before? It must be a song she knew well, but she couldn't quite place it.

It was only as Vicki began to sing that she realised the awful truth. They had both chosen the same song.

Except it wasn't the same, because the backing tape was completely different and the way Vicki was singing it, you would hardly be able to recognise it if you didn't know it well. But there was no doubt about it; it was definitely the same song. What's more, Vicki's version was mind-blowing. She was taking it nearly twice as fast as Evie, launching into a series of complicated dance steps as she sang and moving all over the stage. The delighted audience tapped their feet in time with the rhythm.

It was Ben's fault. He was supposed to have the master list of entries and if two people had entered the same song he should have spotted it. Anyway, even if the judges realised it was a genuine mistake, how on earth was Evie going to follow such a performance? Her own tape didn't allow for such an interpretation; it was only half the speed. Coming immediately after Vicki she couldn't possibly sound anything more than mediocre, an amateur who had got into the second round by mistake. Now she understood why no two competitors were allowed to sing the same song.

Vicki was receiving her verdict from the judges.

'A lovely style, I think' said the Greenlands music teacher and Mr Barraclough nodded, adding 'Good command of the high notes.'

'You look great too,' was Shelley's comment, 'Fab dress, and where did you get your hair done?'

'My mum did it,' said Vicki, smiling diffidently and fidgeting with one of her earrings.

Vernon's turn. 'Interesting choice of song,' he said. 'Not one I would have chosen, but then it's normally sung at half that speed, isn't it? Usually a song I hate, but I must say the way you did it was quite different.'

Evie's heart sank even further into her boots. Could she back out now? But already Ben was saying her name and beckoning her forward. She climbed over the audience, giving a despairing look at Vicki as they came face to face at the front.

'You'll be great,' whispered Vicki as she passed. 'They're not that bad.'

Sue took the backing tape from her and slotted it into the machine.

It took about thirty seconds of the song for the audience to realise they were being given a rerun of the previous number. At first they restricted themselves to murmuring and shuffling but before long some of them erupted into some quite plainly audible comments.

'Oi! Haven't we already had this one?'

'She's nicked Vicki's song!'

'What a nerve.'

'Thought it was against the rules.'

'Shush,' said Ben from his chairman's seat. 'Give the girl a chance.' He was looking very perplexed and rummaging through the papers on the desk in front of him. The teacher from Greenlands leaned across and whispered in his ear and he frowned, then nodded.

Evie, already well into the number, watched all this in desperation from the front as she sang. There was no going back now. Maybe she couldn't move as well as Vicki, but she was going to give it all she could. Vicki's strength had been dancing; Evie's was her voice. Throwing her inhibitions to the wind she threw herself into the song, allowing her voice to glide up and down the scale and to linger on every note. Her backing track wasn't so bad. It had a mesmerising beat, and if she could perform it as differently as possible from Vicki, perhaps she would still be in with a chance. She cradled the microphone in her hands and summoned all her energy to project herself. Across the floor she could see Adam in the back row. He was leaning forward, mouthing encouragement, willing her to do well.

She came to the end and there was a momentary hiatus. The audience seemed to be unsure what response was required. A trickle of applause began from Adam and Dave's row, but at the same time someone said loudly, 'Couldn't you get your own song?'

There was a brief silence, then another voice joined in, 'Yeah, second-rate Stannie! Even have to pinch Greenlands' material!'

This was too much for some of the Stanworth pupils and one or two started to retaliate.

'We don't have to take this from you!' called Brooksie from the corner.

'Yeah, you're just jealous!' joined in Jade.

'Jealous of what? Lack of talent?' retorted a Greenlands boy.

'Why don't you get a life?'

'Why don't you get a song?'

'Hey, hang on a minute, fellas,' exclaimed Ben, but his voice was drowned out by the growing sound of insults flying back and forth. The judges watched nervously, unable to pass their final opinion in the escalating noise. Evie, realising she would have to wait for their verdict, scrambled back to her seat.

'Why on earth didn't you check with Vicki about—?' Adam began to ask her, but was cut off mid-sentence by a round orange missile hurtling past his face.

Brooksie, perched on a stool by the bar, had taken the general breakdown of law and order as a signal to launch an attack on the Greenlands pupils. Looking round for ammunition, the first thing that came to hand was a large box of overripe fruit waiting to be turned into smoothies. He carefully selected a mouldy tangerine and hurled it across the room.

'What the—?' The Greenlands boy caught the full force of the tangerine on his shoulder where it exploded, leaving a sticky orange trail down his school blazer. Scooping up the mushy remains he hurled it straight back at Brooksie, missing him completely but scoring a direct hit on one of the Stanworth girls sitting beside him.

Without hesitation she pulled the fruit box across the bar, rifled though it and brought out a blackening banana. With great deliberation she stripped the peel off and flung it into the Greenlands group. It landed harmlessly enough on the floor, but the battle lines had been drawn.

'Yeah! Fruit fight!' The cry went up.

Within seconds fruit began to fly across the room in all directions, some of it innocuously hitting the walls and floor but much of it reaching the intended targets, leaving puddles of juice and squelchy flesh on clothes and bodies. The air filled with the heady tang of strawberries, mangoes and passion fruit.

Complete mayhem ensued.

'Hey, guys!' called Ben, struggling in vain to make his voice heard above the noise. It was evident he had no chance of regaining control so he pushed Shelley towards Sue, gesticulating to her and the other judges to make a quick escape by the back entrance. Meanwhile he, Noah and the remaining adults did their best to deal with the bedlam. The judges followed Sue in haste, ducking and weaving to avoid low flying projectiles as they went.

Almost at the rear door and behind the rest of the adults, Vernon Eastwood turned back. Watching him, Evie realised he had forgotten his jacket; it was still draped round the chair at the table where he and the other judges had been sitting. He shouted something to Noah, but his voice was lost in the sound of cheerful insults and booing between the two schools. There was nothing for it; he would have to go back for it.

He had only taken one step towards the table when a stray kiwi fruit caught him on the nose, dislodging his eye patch. Instantly, his hand flew to his face, but he was not quick enough. Those standing near him could see his uncovered eye quite clearly. It was exactly the same as the right one. The pair of them moved in total unison, not a hint of glass in sight.

Thrusting an arm over his face he pushed his way through to the table to retrieve his jacket, and then made his exit through the rear entrance as fast as the general chaos would allow.

'Did you see that?' Dave yelled to Evie over the commotion. 'Did you see his eye?'

She nodded. 'What a cheat! It was all a scam to make him look more scary!'

Dave dodged as a pear whistled past. 'No need ever to be frightened of him again!'

The battle raged on. Some of the combatants had run out of fruit, but undeterred they turned to cushions for ammunition. Feathers mingled with strawberry pulp as Greenlands School and Stanworth High worked out their differences in the only way they knew.

***

'Hey, guys!' Tom jerked his head warningly at the main entrance of the club.

The community policeman was standing in the doorway surveying the scene. Another policeman in sergeant's uniform stood beside him.

There was a sudden lull in the noise as one by one the brawlers caught sight of them until at last the room was filled with silence.

The sergeant turned to his colleague. 'Well, PC Carter,' he said reaching for his notebook and pencil. 'What have we here?' His face was set in an expression of unyielding severity, although watching him carefully Evie had the strangest impression that his eyes contained a hint of laughter.

'Looks like a case of serious civil disorder to me, Sergeant Walters.'

'Dear, oh dear, oh dear. The young people of today.' The second policeman gave a great sigh and shook his head sadly. 'Bunch of hooligans.' He caught Brooksie by the sleeve. 'Look at this young fellow, Constable Carter. Have you ever seen such a mess?' Brooksie wiped a strawberry smear from his cheek, doing his best to avoid the constable's eye.

The sergeant wrote in his notebook, and looked around the room. 'Who's in charge here?'

Ben stepped forward. 'Me. I'm sorry, Officer, we were having a competition and things got a bit out of hand...'

'I should say they did. PC Carter here has had his walkie-talkie jammed with all the complaints from shopkeepers in the area. Had to call me in as backup. Your club's getting a bad name round here, you know.'

'I know, and I'm sorry. It won't happen again.'

'I should hope not.' He strolled round the room, pausing from time to time to peer more thoroughly at the more offensive items of greengrocery, all the while making notes in his book. PC Carter followed at his elbow.

'This is a nasty incident,' said Sergeant Walters after a while, 'a very nasty incident indeed. Not good at all. It'll have to go down in the records, you know.'

He tapped his chin reflectively with his pencil. No one spoke.

'Well, maybe we won't follow it up this time. Looks like you've got a lot of cleaning up to do to keep yourselves busy.' He turned to Ben. 'I should get these young people onto it if I were you.'

'Certainly will, Officer.'

'Perhaps it would be safer to keep your fruit under lock and key in future?'

'I guess it would, Officer.'

'And may I suggest you have more adults present next time you plan an event like this?'

'Will do, Officer. Thank you.'

***

Evie, armed with a mop and bucket, cleaned a patch of floor next to Vicki.

'I didn't mean to pinch your song. I just didn't know.'

Vicki scrubbed at a patch of trodden-in blueberries. 'You could have checked.'

'Yes, but you were so secretive. How was I to guess?'

'Didn't Ben tell you when you borrowed the tape?'

'No. To be fair, because the backing groups were different, perhaps he just didn't realise.'

'The titles were the same,' pointed out Vicki.

'Yes, but I think they were listed by the name of the singer. Anyway, you don't really think I'd have done it on purpose, do you?'

'S'pose not.' She was quiet for a moment, then she stopped rubbing the floor and sat back on her heels looking at her friend.

'What...?' began Evie, then she caught Vicki's eye. She began to laugh.

'Fruit fighting,' snorted Vicki. 'What a great idea. Totally inspired. It ought to be an organised club activity.'

'Strictly with parental consent, of course,' chuckled Evie. 'Forms to be signed and everything. Dangerous stuff, fruit.'

'Weapons of mass destruction in the wrong hands,' agreed Vicky gravely.

'Haven't had such fun in ages.'

'Those policemen. Were they serious?'

'Can't have been. The whole thing was a wind-up.'

'And did you see Vernon Eastwood? Nothing wrong with his eye at all. Had us all fooled.'

'What a poser!'

They scrubbed away side by side, replaying the whole event to each other, giggling intermittently as they worked.

'But seriously, Vick, do you think I'll have been disqualified?' said Evie rubbing an itchy nose with a dishclothy hand.

'Your song was really good,' her friend reassured her. 'If you ask me they'll keep you in.'

'Even though I've broken the rules?'

'You haven't broken them on purpose. Anyway. If you've broken them, so've I. Which means we'll both be disqualified. Does that make you feel any better?'

'Kind of. All for one, one for all. But maybe it won't come to that.'

'Who knows? Guess it depends on the judges. They're all pretty reasonable.'

'Except Vernon,' Evie reminded her.

'Oh yes, I was forgetting him. Except Vernon, then. But then don't worry, Ben'll be on our side.'

'Course he will. And at least we had a laugh.'

'Didn't we just?'

Seven

Evie wasn't left in suspense for long. She was sitting in an English lesson the following Monday morning when the mobile in her skirt pocket started juddering. There was a very strict rule about mobiles being on during lessons but she always left it on 'vibrate' in case her dad tried to text her from work. Keeping one eye on Mrs Green scrawling notes on the board about the Romantic poets and nature, Evie slid her phone out of her pocket into her lap under the table where she could read it without being seen from the front.

Ben's name had appeared at the top of the message list.

Good news. Ring me asap. Ben

The rest of her morning passed in a frenzy of impatience until the lunchtime pips sounded and she was free to find a corner of the playing field and call him.

'Ben? It's me, Evie. I got your message.'

'Hope I didn't disturb a lesson or anything.'

'Just English Lit. Wordsworth. But my phone was on vibrate.'

'Ah, yes. "I wandered lonely as a cloud..."'

'Per-lease. That's so-o Primary School. We're doing stuff about the poets and nature. But I guess you didn't text me for an English lesson?'

'No, course not. I just had John Barraclough on the phone about last Friday's fiasco.'

'Don't tell me. They want to abandon the whole contest.'

'Not at all. They were very impressed by the standard of entrants in the second round.'

'Except me, I s'pose. They didn't even get the chance to discuss my song, and anyway I did the same one as Vicki, so I guess that's that.' She still squirmed at the memory.

'That's where you're wrong. They *did* like your song, and that's why John Barraclough rang me. Obviously they left rather more speedily than expected, but he and the other judges continued their discussion in the car park and the upshot was they decided you should go on to the final round. So you're still in, Evie!'

Evie let out a squeal. Two passing Year Eights, deep in an intense discussion, stopped gabbing for a moment and gave her a very strange look.

'You're not making it up? I can't believe it! I was so sure I'd blown it.'

'Why would you think that? It wasn't your fault you and Vicki picked the same song. Anyway, there wasn't anything in the rules about whether you could pick the same song if each had a different backing. I guess if anyone was to blame it was me, but because they were on two separate tapes, I just never made the connection.'

'But what about the whole flying fruit incident? Surely that was enough to make them give up on the entire thing?'

'Not at all. In fact, I think, between you and me, a couple of the judges were quite amused by it. From what John said about Shelley, for two pins she'd have been in there, chucking satsumas with the rest of you.' He chuckled quietly for a moment but then his voice became very stern. 'Not that I condone such behaviour in any way. We have enough trouble keeping on the right side of the locals as it is, without my having complaints from the neighbours and visits from the police. Not to mention the hours cleaning up the mess afterwards. There was no excuse for it at all. If you Stannie kids can't come to some sort of truce with the

Greenlands mob, I can't think how the club can go on running peacefully.'

'I know, Ben. But they've always been like that.'

'What's all this "they"? You're one of them. It's up to each person to act maturely. If everyone took some responsibility – irrespective of which school they go to – perhaps the problem wouldn't arise.'

Evie waited patiently for the lecture to finish. 'So we're going ahead with the third round as planned?'

'Not quite as planned. The judges felt Halfway House was too conducive to misbehaviour, so they've stipulated it must be in the Town Hall where things can be kept under better control. In fact, there'll be more room in there so it might work out better anyway. We never expected the contest to be quite the crowd-puller it's turned out to be.'

Evie tried to visualise the final round in the hall. 'It won't be so good. The atmosphere there'll be all wrong.'

'I know. But beggars can't be choosers. We're just lucky it hasn't been cancelled altogether. Anyway, must go, work to do.'

'Yeah, sure. Thanks for letting me know, Ben.'

'No worries. And Evie.'

'Yes?'

'Get yourself an original song, this time, eh? For me?'

***

'So. Into Round Three, are we? I'm impressed. Not that I didn't think you could do it. Who's on the final list, then?'

Dave was looking decidedly hot. He was wearing a new dark blue shirt which contrasted very satisfyingly with the light gold sun streaks in his hair and which made all the other boys in the club look distinctly naff in their droopy school shirts and tatty blazers. Evie grinned at him happily from her barstool perch and made slurpy noises as she drained the dregs of her strawberry smoothie. Not for the first time, she wondered why a fit lad like him would bother with a girl like her.

'Well, there's Vicki, and that girl called Hannah who goes to St Margaret's, the very tall girl with curly hair. Then there's Martin Fraser from your college and Paul, you know, the guy who sings so well? He has to be the top favourite – you can see they all love him. And then there's me and that's it. Just five of us.'

'And when is it?'

'Beginning of next term. We've got the whole Easter break to practise, and I think this time Adam's really got a good song for me.'

'Cool. So you're going to be a bit freer for a while then?'

'If you mean, have I got to rehearse, no, not until the song's written. If you mean, have I got loads of homework, yes, I have. But nothing that can't wait. Why?'

Dave shifted his weight fractionally on his stool. 'It's just an idea I had. My mum and dad and little sister are going away next weekend to see my auntie in York. I can't go, 'cause I've got a match in the afternoon. Anyway, it's totally and completely dead boring at my auntie's house, no one my age and nothing to do. They've said I can stay at home on my own. So I was wondering...'

'Wondering?'

'...Wondering whether you might like to come over for the evening on Saturday. I could cook you a special meal, I saw this Jamie Oliver recipe on telly which I reckon I could do with those pasta tube things, and we could watch a DVD or something...?'

'What, just you and me? No one else?'

'Well it'd be very cosy, wouldn't it? No one to interrupt.' He looked straight into her eyes. 'If you see what I mean?'

Evie did indeed see what he meant. She took the straw out of her glass and examined it carefully. 'But wouldn't your parents object?'

'They wouldn't know, would they? And what they didn't know, wouldn't hurt.' He watched steadily for her reaction. 'You could even tell your dad you were staying the night with a friend and then there'd be no trouble about what time you had to get home.'

Any doubts she may have had previously were completely dispelled by this last suggestion. There was no mistaking what he had in mind.

She wriggled a little. 'I don't know. I might have extra coursework or something. I need to think about it...' How lame did that sound?

''Course, if you're scared, forget it. Or perhaps you don't really like me?'

She stared at the little golden hairs on the back of his suntanned wrist. 'It's not that. You know I like you. It's just...'

'Or are you frightened that you might, you know, that something might happen to you? You needn't worry, I'll look after it.'

Evie hadn't actually thought that far, but now Dave had mentioned it with such apparent confidence, she couldn't help wondering how many other girls he'd made such a suggestion to.

But she did like him. Very much. If it was going to be with anyone, now, at this stage in her life, it could only be with Dave. And yet...

Her mother had always told her to wait. That there would be one special person and that he would be worth waiting for. That you could only build happy families on commitment between partners for a lifetime. That meant marriage, didn't it? But her mother had grown up in another age, a time when people didn't have a new partner every week, a time when marriage was the accepted thing. Life was different in the new millennium; nobody stuck to the old rules any more. What harm could it possibly do to show someone how much you like them? She couldn't bring herself to use the word 'love' when thinking about Dave; it seemed too big a term to use when her main reason for liking him so much was to do with his drop-dead gorgeous looks.

'I don't know,' she said again.

'Hey, you two!' Adam bounced up. 'Have you seen the new notice on the board? Ben's planning a Halfway House outing to *Heaven Alive*.' Adam had fully recovered from the flu and seemed more cheerful than he had been for some time.

'What's *Heaven Alive*?' asked Dave.

'It's a Christian event – happens every two months at the Queen's Theatre in Birmingham. All the big Christian bands and drama and interactive stuff and always a really good speaker. You'd love it,' Evie told him.

'I'm definitely going,' said Adam. 'I'm hoping Tom might come too.'

'Sounds a bit heavy. Would it be all Jesus talk?' Dave wanted to know.

'Well, obviously a Christian event is going to make you think about that sort of thing,' said Adam, guardedly. 'Otherwise it wouldn't be different from any other pop concert. But nobody's going to *force* you into anything.'

Dave was looking at Evie. 'Well, Evie?' he said. 'I guess it all depends on you. We can either do, you know, the thing I suggested for Saturday night, or we could go to *Heaven Alive*. I know which I'd prefer,' he added.

Evie was silent for a moment. Her chief reaction was mild relief; the trip to Birmingham would provide her with a cast-iron excuse for postponing any kind of decision about taking her relationship with Dave to a new level. Perhaps God had even especially sent it for this reason.

But even as she started to reply, Adam interrupted. 'What "thing" had you suggested?' he asked.

'I don't see that it's really any of your business,' replied Dave calmly. 'It's just between me and Evie.'

'But is it something you could do some other time? It'd be a real shame to miss this.'

'No it's not,' said Dave shortly.

'Well, what then? Is it a party or something?'

'If you must know, Evie and I were planning a quiet evening together at my house. We just want to have some time alone. OK?'

'But you can do that any time. Besides, it won't be very quiet with your parents and sister around.'

'They won't be there. They're going to York,' blurted out Evie.

'Oh,' said Adam. Then again, but this time with dawning understanding, 'Oh.'

'Don't look at me like that,' said Evie, wriggling under his expression of ferocious disapproval. 'It's nothing to do with you. It's my own life, and I can do what I want.'

'She's right,' put in Dave.

'You'll regret it,' said Adam, completely ignoring him and speaking urgently to Evie. 'He's not right for you. Can't you see it, Evie? Good looks aren't everything, it's who the person is that matters, and he's not what you think he is. You don't have anything in common.'

''Course we have,' said Evie indignantly. 'We like some of the same music and... and... stuff...' her voice trailed away lamely.

'See what I mean? You're my best mate, Eves, the most special person I know. Don't go and throw yourself away just 'cause he's got a pretty face. And what about your Christian faith? Does that count for nothing?'

'Kid's stuff. Indoctrination,' laughed Dave. 'Grow up, Adam.'

'You know what he wants, Evie, don't you? And when he's got it he won't be interested in you any more. Believe me, I know.'

Suddenly Evie lost her temper. She felt as if a white light had exploded in her head. 'Oh yes, you know, do you, Adam? With all your enormous experience of girls and relationships? You think you can tell me what's right and what's wrong? What makes you into such a know-all? You've never even had a girlfriend!'

'That doesn't stop me from seeing things. Evie, listen to me, if you do this, I'll... I'll...' he cast around wildly for the thing that would make the biggest impact. 'I'll tell your dad!'

Evie stared at him. 'You wouldn't.'

'I would. It'd be in your best interests.'

This was so completely out of character that for a moment she was speechless. She was sure he didn't mean it, but why was he so upset?

And then at last she said the words that had been lurking in her head for several weeks. 'Adam Kendall. Are you by any chance jealous?'

For a second or two he stared back at her, the blood draining from his face. Then without a word he scooped up his school blazer from the floor and walked out of the club.

There was a long silence.

A whole range of disturbing thoughts fought for supremacy in Evie's head. So it was true, Adam really did like her in that way. All his histrionics had been because he wanted her for himself. How could she not have realised? It was just that they had been like brother and sister all their lives and it had never occurred to her that he could ever think of her in any other way. Even now the whole idea seemed peculiarly unlikely, as if somehow it didn't fit with the Adam she knew. Yet the evidence was there. No one could have missed the way he went so pale when she accused him of being jealous.

Dave was speaking to her. 'So can I take that as a yes?'

Evie dragged herself back to reality. 'What? What do you mean? Yes to what?'

'Yes, you'll come over on Saturday night. That's what you said to Adam.'

'Did I?' She wasn't sure that she had. But all of a sudden she just wanted the whole thing over and done with. She took a deep breath. 'All right. Saturday night at your place it is. I'll think of something to tell Dad. I'm sure Adam won't really say anything.'

Dave smiled, a heart-melting smile, right into her eyes. 'Good choice. You'll be glad you did. Take no notice of Adam, we're going to have a great time.' He put his hand on hers and squeezed it. She had a great longing to feel his arms round her, but would have to be content with this for the moment. Snogging was strictly off-limits at Halfway House.

***

She walked down the hill towards her home, her mind racing round in circles. Had she made the wrong decision? How was she ever going to regain her friendship with Adam? She needed to talk to Vicki, someone her own age with her own beliefs.

'Do I smell or something?'

She had almost completely passed by without noticing Jade who was sitting on the wall by the bus station, smoking a cigarette and swinging her legs.

'What's the big hurry?' asked Jade. 'You look as though you've just been struck by lightning. Something wrong?'

Jade was the last person Evie wanted to confide in at that moment, yet the urge to talk to anyone at all was even stronger than the gut feeling that she ought to walk on. She stopped and put her school files on the wall and swung herself up next to Jade.

'Sorry. Stuff on my mind.'

Jade took a drag from her cigarette, fingered the stud in her tongue and looked sideways at her. 'Lad trouble?' she asked sympathetically.

'And how.'

'Tell your Auntie Jade.'

Out it all came. About how she really liked Dave and how she couldn't decide if she wanted to go further with their relationship. About how Adam had reacted so weirdly to her seeing Dave and how she'd begun to suspect that maybe Adam liked her. About how Dave had suggested the meal at his place...

'Hang on, hang on,' interrupted Jade. 'Are you saying you've never done it with anyone else? Like Dave would be the first?'

'No. I mean yes. Dave would be the first.'

'And you really like him?'

'Yes, course I do. Wouldn't anyone?'

'That's true enough. In fact, I'll have him if you don't want him. So what's the problem?'

'It might not seem a problem to you but it is to me.' Evie knew Jade had slept with loads of guys; at least that was what she had led everyone to believe (although Evie sometimes suspected there were fewer than Jade claimed).

'My problem is a) do I really want to do this when part of me believes it's wrong? And b) what do I do about Adam? If he really does like me – you know, in that way – what am I supposed to do about it? Is this the end of a lifetime's friendship?'

Jade blew out a curl of smoke. 'Well, let's start with the Dave thing. Seems to me if you like a bloke you might as well do it. Otherwise he'll just go and find someone else who's got less hang-ups.'

'That's no reason for sleeping with someone,' said Evie, shocked.

'Oh, come on, Eves, we're talking fellas here. Don't know what kind of world you've been living in all your life, but its certainly nothing like mine. Bottom line: guys want sex. That's what it's all about.'

'But what about love and commitment and everything?'

Jade snorted. 'That's just a line they give you at Sunday school to keep you from having too much excitement. Anyway, take it from me, sex is fun.'

Evie looked doubtful. 'I don't know. Suppose everyone took that line. Not the "sex is fun" bit, I'll take your word for that, but the "if you like someone you might as well do it" thing. Supposing the person you want to do it with is married, for example?' The image of her dad holding hands with Adam's mum had just flitted unbidden into her head.

'Oh, well it's different if you're *married*. That's why I'd never get married. Who wants to be tied down to someone you might get bored with?' Jade swung her legs nonchalantly.

'So you think it's OK for me to go ahead with Dave?' Strangely, this conversation was causing her to have bigger doubts than she'd had before.

'Why not? Most girls'd give their back teeth to have a chance with him. I know I would,' said Jade.

'And what about Adam? What do I do about him? He really hates me going out with Dave.'

Jade threw her cigarette on the ground, jumped off the wall and stubbed it out with her school shoe. She was laughing quietly.

'What's so funny?' asked Evie, puzzled. 'Have I said something stupid?'

'Oh, Evie,' chortled Jade, 'you're such an innocent! Haven't you worked it out yet?'

'Of course I have. I told you, it's obvious Adam fancies me. That's why he's so moody all the time, he's jealous. I'm not completely stupid.'

'Oh, but you are completely stupid. Listen, and I'll tell you what everyone else worked out ages ago. We could all see it at the Llanwellyn weekend. You're half right. Yes, Adam's jealous, jealous as hell, but not of Dave.'

'What do you mean? Who else is there to be jealous of?'

'It's not you he fancies, petal, more's the pity. At least that would be relatively uncomplicated.'

And then, suddenly, Evie knew what Jade was going to say.

'The only person Adam's interested in is Dave.'

Eight

'Adam's gay.'

The words were out of Evie's mouth before she'd fully grasped their significance. Surely it couldn't be true.

There had never been a day in her life when Adam hadn't been her friend. Wouldn't she have known? Wouldn't he have told her something as important as this? And yet, in the same moment she realised there were some things you couldn't share with even your closest friends – at least, not if you weren't sure of the reception they would receive.

She said slowly, 'You must be wrong. Not Adam. I'd know.' It had to be some kind of stupid joke; exactly the sort of thing you'd expect from Jade.

'It's not just me who thinks so. Ask anyone. Why do you think he's so uninterested in girls?'

'But he is. I'm his best friend, and I'm a girl.'

'Ah yes, but "friend" is the crucial word there, isn't it? You said yourself you couldn't imagine it being anything else. Why not? He's not bad-looking.'

Evie eased herself down off the wall. 'I think you're sick. Sick and perverted. I'm going home now.'

Jade grinned. 'Who's sick and perverted? Seems to me like it's you. *I* don't have any trouble with Adam being gay. I know loads of people like him, most of them really nice. What difference does it make whether they like doing it with guys or girls?'

'Yes, but it's not right...' Evie started to protest, but stopped mid-sentence. She didn't really know what she thought.

'They're still *people*, aren't they? I'd have thought you out of everyone would be the first to say you should love everyone. Like a good little Christian.'

'I do love everyone! At least I try to.' Evie was having some difficulty in loving Jade right at this moment. 'And I don't mind what everyone else does, it's just—'

'Just your precious Adam? You want to keep him in a nice little box where you can keep an eye on what he's up to? You thought you knew him and now you find you don't? Growing up time, Evie.'

'But it's in the Bible...' Evie faltered.

'Oh, spare me! I've been around you church freaks long enough to know that half the stuff in the Bible was only meant for cavemen and dinosaurs. It's the twentieth century now, babe!'

'Twenty-first,' said Evie, mechanically.

'Whatever. We see things in a civilised way now, women have the vote and you can do what you want as long as it doesn't hurt anyone. 'S'gotta be right. You know, it's people like you who cause religious wars and stuff, with all your rules and hang-ups. Like not eating bacon,' she added inconsequentially. 'That's *gotta* be wrong. Imagine life without bacon!'

'I think that's a Jewish thing,' said Evie, somewhat confused, but Jade had been distracted by the approach of her bus and was gathering herself together.

'Well, I don't see what the problem is. Ask Adam, if you wanna be sure. I s'pect he'll tell you if you ask outright. It really isn't a big deal, Evie. Don't get your knickers in such a twist.' She hopped up on the platform of the bus, rummaging in her blazer pocket for her fare. 'But I wouldn't give him all that "Bible-says" stuff if you want to stay friends. That's my advice, if you're interested, which I don't s'pose you are. Byee!'

Evie walked slowly down the road towards her house. Her dad would be waiting for her at home. He was going out to some meeting to do with work, but he'd promised to cook her an early meal before he went. She really didn't feel like speaking to him just at that moment. In fact she didn't really feel like speaking to anyone.

Jade was right. The only way to clear this up was to talk to Adam. She would go there now.

She fumbled in her bag for her mobile. 'Dad? I'm going to be a bit late. Something I have to do... No, it can't wait. Can you leave my dinner in the oven?'

A minute later she was walking away from her road and towards Adam's house.

His mum, Julie answered the door. 'Evie! I wasn't expecting you. Adam never said you were coming round. He's upstairs somewhere, probably in his room. Do you want to go and find him?' She lowered her voice and added, 'Something happened at Halfway House today. He's in a dreadful state, won't talk to me at all. Do you know anything about it?'

Evie nodded. 'Yes, I have a fair idea what's wrong. I'll go and talk to him if that's OK.'

Adam's bedroom was at the back of the house, across the landing from Tom's. There was a nameplate on his door, a little yellow car with big wide-open eyes and a smiley radiator and ADAM painted in curly letters across the top of the windscreen. Underneath was a poster, almost entirely black except for a rising mushroom cloud and the word 'DEATH' printed in blood red down the right hand-side.

Evie knocked gently on the door. There was no reply. She banged harder. Tom looked out from the room opposite but she ignored him and banged again.

'Who is it?' Adam's voice sounded muffled.

'Me, Evie.'

There was a pause, then the door opened a crack and Adam peered out. He had taken off his shoes and sweater and his school shirt hung out round his hips. A smell of unwashed socks wafted onto the landing.

'Can I come in?'

'S'pose so.' He pulled the door wider.

Evie walked past him and deposited her school bag on the bed. He stood by the door watching her.

'Why did you run off like that?' she demanded to know.

Adam didn't reply, instead going over to his CD player and inserting a disc. The room began to throb with a hypnotic beat.

'Ad, I'm talking to you! What's going on? What've I done to upset you?'

'Nothing.' He sat on the chair in front of the chest of drawers that doubled up as a desk and started rearranging his CD collection, his back firmly turned towards her.

'*Adam*. This is me, Evie!'

'OK.' He dumped a pile of CDs on the shelf and swivelled round to face her. 'Whaddya wanna know?'

'I want to know why you're acting so strange about me and Dave. I want to know if it's just that you don't like Dave or whether you're trying to protect me, or if it's something else.'

'Something else? Like what?'

'Jade says...' she stopped.

'What does Jade say?' His face was impassive.

'Jade says – look Ad, don't get me wrong, I don't believe this for a moment, you know what Jade's like, judges everyone by her own wacky ideas.'

'What does Jade say?'

'She says that the reason you're so upset about my relationship with Dave is because – this is only what Jade says, not me, you understand – she says it's because you

98

fancy him yourself.' She waited for his response. None was forthcoming, so she blundered on, 'Which is hilarious when you come to think about it. I mean. You? With Dave? Like that? As if.'

Adam leaned forward and put his head in his hands.

'Ad, say something.'

'What can I say?'

'That it's all rubbish, of course! That Jade made the whole thing up! That I should mind my own business and that you're seeing six girls a week! At least don't sit there saying nothing as if it was all true!'

He lifted his head and looked straight at her. 'But it is all true.'

She sat on the bed heavily. 'Oh, Adam.'

For a moment neither of them spoke. Then Evie said 'But why...? When...? How long...?'

He looked away from her, twisting his tie into knots in his hands and started to speak very quickly.

'I've known for ages I wasn't like most of the other guys at school. At least since I was 13 or 14, maybe even younger. I didn't even know why I felt different to begin with; I just thought maybe I'd got a bit left behind. You know, like when they were all kidding around about girls and stuff, I just wasn't interested. Do you remember that picture Brooksie had at school, and he was getting people to give him 50p a go to have a look?'

Evie nodded mutely. She hadn't seen the actual picture but she had a pretty good idea of the sort of thing that was in it. Mr Phillips had caught some of the lads cackling over it and had torn it up, as she remembered.

'Well, I had a look at that and it did nothing for me. Nothing.'

'Yes, but that doesn't mean...'

'Then I started looking at stuff on the Internet. I really didn't want to but I couldn't help it. And I found it wasn't the women I wanted to look at.'

Evie resisted the urge to put her fingers in her ears. She didn't want to hear any more.

'I started to think about, you know, what it was going to mean to my whole life if this was who I was. There was that talk in church last autumn – remember? – when the vicar said that stuff about how it was wrong for a Christian to be a practising gay. How could I go on being a Christian if this was the way I felt?'

'Did you tell anyone?'

'No. If I was going to tell anyone it would probably have been you. It was as if I was living one life on the outside and a completely different one on the inside.

'And then Dave came along. He was good-looking and funny and strong and the first person I'd met who I really wanted to have a proper relationship with. I mean, not just the physical thing, but a serious friendship; someone I could tell everything to and be myself with. He was the first *guy* I'd felt like that about. But you got in before I had a chance. It was you he wanted to be with, not me.' The tie in his hands was full of little knots from his absent-minded fidgeting, and now he was abstractedly trying to undo them. 'I don't even know if the vicar's right. I mean, there's gay people everywhere. On the telly, that late-night thing on Saturday, you know the one I mean?'

'Not my bag, I'm afraid,' said Evie.

'Well, it's on every week. All the gay celebrities come on and talk about their lives. It's an accepted thing. And *Will and Grace*.'

'Yes, but Ad, just because it's on telly that doesn't make it right.'

'Certainly doesn't,' said a voice from the doorway. They both looked up. Tom was standing there, his hands on his hips, his face wrinkled up in an expression of disgust. Adam swore quietly to himself.

'Tom! How long have you been listening?' said Evie in alarm.

'Long enough to get the picture. The whole disgusting perverted picture.'

'Tom—'

But now the floodgates were open nothing would stop him.

'I might've known, he's always been a big girl. All these groups here...' he waved a hand at the boy bands on posters lining the bedroom walls, 'I shoulda realised they were all too pretty to be there just 'cause he liked their music. Only thing that's missing is pink flowery wallpaper!'

Evie opened her mouth in protest, but Tom went on, 'All that religion. Off to church on Sundays, Mummy's little treasure, just the little boy she always wanted. All I get is. "Don't put dirty feet on the chair, Tom, Mummy will have to clean it. Help Mummy with the washing-up, Tom, she's had a long day." Diddums. Does Mummy know what you really are?' He shook his head in mock disbelief. 'My brother, eh. My little brother, a poof. I'm related to a fairy.'

Adam's eyes blazed. 'Oh yeah? Well, at least I'm a fairy who cares about people! All you ever think about is football and beer and the next girl you're going to get it on with!'

'Normal activities, mate, normal activities. Whereas you're *ab*normal, you big freak.'

'Get out,' said Adam, so quietly it was almost a whisper. His face was deathly white.

'Don't worry, pal, I'm going to. Out to see my normal friends. Breathe a bit of fresh air.' Tom turned to the door, then paused. 'By the way, I'd be grateful if you didn't mention your – what shall I call it – *preferences*, around my friends. Be a bit embarrassing if they thought I was the same. Know what I mean?'

'Out!'

'OK, OK, I'm off. Cheerio.'

Adam turned to Evie, rage burning in his face. 'And you! Coming round here and preaching to me!'

'But Ad, that's not true—'

'Oh, don't think I didn't see it in your eyes! You're no better than him. You and your Christian claptrap! Don't think I don't know you're planning to sleep with Dave! The only reason you haven't done it so far is 'cause you're scared! You stand there and lecture me about what's right and what's wrong and you can't even work it out in your own life.'

'I'm not judging you, Adam, really I'm not—'

'Oh yeah? Don't give me that! I saw the way you looked when I told you about the Internet. You think I'm a pervert, just like Tom does! It's just that you dress it all up in Christianity while he comes straight out with what he feels without trying to hide behind religion. Why don't you just take your holier-than-thou attitude and stuff it where the sun don't shine?'

The CD came to an end and the thudding beat faded away to nothing.

'If that's really what you think, I'll go,' said Evie, quietly. She picked up her bag from the bed. 'I always thought we were friends. That we told each other everything.' Tears were perilously close.

'Yeah, well. A lot of what you thought turns out to be wrong, doesn't it?' said Adam bitterly.

Adam's mum was waiting at the bottom of the stairs to see her out. 'What on earth's going on up there?' she asked anxiously. 'All that shouting? I thought you must be having a terrible row.'

But Evie was crying now and couldn't look her in the eye. 'Ask Adam,' she said, miserably. 'He'll tell you.' Blindly, she fumbled for the front door handle.

'Evie, won't you tell me what's wrong?' Julie was all concern.

'Can't. Not up to me. Ask Adam. Gotta get home to Dad. Tea's waiting.'

'Is it about your song? Is it that you can't agree about it?'

'No, no, nothing like that,' sniffed Evie. 'Talk to you later. See you.' She stepped out into the evening sunshine, half blinded by tears.

Until Julie mentioned it she'd forgotten all about the song. Goodness only knew what would happen about that now.

***

Her dad had already left for his meeting by the time she got home. There was a dried-up chicken pie in the oven and a precariously balanced bowl of mashed potato acting as a lid on a dish of overcooked greens. Evie pulled everything off the shelf, opened the rubbish bin and deposited the cabbage into it. Next she put the pie and the potato on a plate and covered the whole thing in tomato ketchup. Pouring herself a glass of water, she put it all on a tray and carried it through to the lounge to eat in front of the TV.

She flipped through the channels despondently. On BBC1 there was a programme about a family who'd left a perfectly good house in Birmingham to go and live on what appeared to be a building site in Spain. The children, three of them, were interviewed in turn and moaned about the weather (too hot), the food (too spicy) and the schools (too Spanish). BBC2 was showing unalleviated snooker and ITV had a programme about crime in the inner cities. Channel 4 was running a repeat of a wildlife programme about elephants in the Masai Mara. Evie decided to go with the elephants.

She had almost finished her meal when the phone rang.

'Evie? It's me.'

'Hi, Dave.'

'What are you doing?'

'Watching a programme about elephants. Did you know that they live pretty much like us? In families and everything? Even to the point of making graveyards.' She'd turned the volume down but left the picture flickering. A group of elephants were drinking at a waterhole.

'Bizarre. Anyway, just wanted to make sure you were OK. You disappeared rather suddenly after Adam went so peculiar. Are you still up for Saturday?'

Evie gripped the receiver tightly. 'Actually, Dave, I'm not really.'

She heard his deep sigh of irritation. 'Why am I not surprised? It's all that stuff Adam said, isn't it?'

'No, it's not that. I just decided it would be a really bad idea.'

'Oh, come on. We've already had this conversation. Surely we haven't got to go through it all over again?'

She kept her eyes on the screen. 'Something's come up, something I wasn't expecting.'

'You mean, you've got to be somewhere else?' She could almost see him tapping his fingers on the phone in exasperation.

'Not exactly.' A baby elephant was nuzzling up to its mother who was passing it great trunkfuls of vegetation. 'I found out something and it made me think differently.'

'For Pete's sake, make up your mind. One minute you're all over me, apparently begging for it, and the next you come over all high-minded and self-righteous. For the last time, do you or don't you want to come over next Saturday?'

'I don't.'

'Fine. Now we know where we stand. I should've guessed you weren't up for it when we went on that weekend. You and all your mates with your Bibles and your God stuff.'

'Dave, I—'

'It's OK, I understand. I'm sure you'll have a great time at "Heavenly Choirs" or "Angel Delight" or whatever it's called.'

'I'm sorry, really I am.' Sorry for what? That she wasn't going to sleep with him? That she and Adam had wanted the same person? That she had ever got into the situation in the first place?

'Forget it. See you around, Evie.'

She turned the volume up again and sat and stared at the TV screen, the remains of her meal uneaten.

It seemed that the elephant family wasn't quite like a human one after all. The women and children all lived together while the males went off and did things on their own, only returning when they wanted to mate.

Men. A law unto themselves.

***

She slept badly and woke with a headache. She would have to face Adam in school today.

It wasn't until break that she ran into him, in front of the lockers, collecting his shoes for PE. His eyes met hers for a minute as he carefully turned the key in the slot, then he picked his trainers up, slammed the door and strode off wordlessly down the corridor. Evie ran after him.

'Ad! Wait a minute! What about the song?'

He walked on.

'Aren't you going to do it? What about me and the final round?'

'What about you and the final round?'

'I can't do it without you! I haven't got a song.'

'Is that right? Excuse me if I don't cry.'

'But Adam, I need you.'

He stopped and turned. 'Oh yes, of course, I was forgetting, you need me. Always about you, isn't it? Well, just at the moment I'm not feeling very creative right now, I'm afraid. You're going to have to manage on your own.'

'But you had such a good idea for a song! You even played me a bit. Don't you even want to try?'

'Just at the moment, Evie, I don't want to try anything. If you want to know, I don't think you and me are such a good team anyway.'

'How can you *say* that?'

'Look, can we talk about this another time? I've got a PE lesson to get to. I'll catch up with you later.'

Evie sat down on the flight of steps beside the lockers and watched him march off towards the gym. She had never felt so depressed in her whole life.

There was no hope for her and Dave now. How could she possibly continue a relationship with him knowing how Adam felt about him? Her friendship with Adam was ruined too; how could she be friends with someone who'd hidden such a big thing from her for so long? Anyway, after all the things he'd said about her being holier-than-thou and two-faced, she didn't think their relationship could ever get back to its old comfortable state. And now she didn't even have a song to sing at the contest.

And besides all that was the persistent niggle at the back of her mind about her dad and Julie, something that still hadn't been resolved. She felt almost certain there was something going on between them now, but had it been going on for years? The thought of uncovering yet another dreadful secret was almost too much to bear. Not for the first time she thought about confronting her dad, but the fear of where it might lead was too great.

Another thought struck her. Even supposing the friendship between her dad and Julie was perfectly innocent and they were only now beginning to be attracted to each other, how would he react to the news that one of her sons was gay? He could be very old-fashioned about that sort of thing. Everything was going horribly wrong.

If only her mum were still around. Of course, she still had Vicki – better than no one she supposed. It was just that Vicki could be a bit unreliable in her advice.

***

But it was Saturday before she saw Vicki. Her friend was waiting for her at the entrance of Halfway House where the group was meeting for the outing to *Heaven Alive*. Several people had already gathered, but there was no sign of Adam.

'Which way did you come?' asked Vicki without preamble. She was obviously struggling to contain some piece of earth-shattering news.

'The usual way. Walked up from home. Why?'

'Did you see them? Just a minute ago?'

'See who?'

Vicki looked slightly uncomfortable, but the urge to share the latest piece of gossip was clearly greater than any desire to protect Evie. 'Dave. With Jade. Going up towards his house. The louse.'

'What?'

'Look! You can still see them. Going up past the health food shop.'

Evie squinted across the road. Dave and Jade were some way away but still recognisable in the distance as they walked up the hill. Dave was in a white T-shirt and blue jeans, instantly identifiable by his easy graceful walk. Jade was dressed to kill in high heels and a very short skirt, her hair spiked up for the occasion, her blouse slipping down over one shoulder.

And Dave's arm was round that shoulder.

Nine

It was several days before Evie plucked up the courage to go back to Halfway House. She thought it was extremely unlikely that Adam would show up there but she couldn't be sure. Worse still was the prospect of bumping into Dave – or even Jade – and having to pretend she didn't know what had been going on. In fact, she reflected ironically, about half of the population of Stanworth were a potential source of major embarrassment.

As predicted, Vicki hadn't been much help when she'd talked to her about Adam. It was as Jade had said: everyone except Evie had already guessed that Adam was gay, Vicki included.

'Why didn't you tell me?' Evie demanded.

'What was the point? It wasn't going to affect you and Dave, was it? It's Adam's problem, not yours.'

'*Of course* it affects me and Dave. I couldn't carry on going out with him after I knew that, could I?' Vicki had some extraordinary blind spots.

'So have you dumped him permanently, then?'

'More like he's dumped me. Anyway, looks like Jade's got him now. The cow. Sorry, Vick, but honestly, she doesn't care what she does to other people's feelings. The whole thing's such a mess.'

The worst part was that she had so nearly slept with Dave. She felt like a person who had offered a priceless gift to someone only to have it trampled in the dust. She wouldn't make that mistake again. She had said nothing to her father about any of what had happened, although he must have guessed something was troubling her from the way she shut herself in her room as soon as she got home every day. That, and the long, morose silences at mealtimes.

She saw both Adam and Jade at school, of course, but it was quite easy to keep out of their way. Adam's timetable was almost completely different from hers and although she and Jade had more lessons that coincided, it was no problem to sit on the other side of the room and avoid eye contact.

On Thursday she got out of school early; Mr Phillips was struck down with a migraine just before the physics lesson and the last two periods of the afternoon were cancelled. There was nowhere to go at that time of day, she had no money and the thought of the empty bungalow and the pile of extra physics homework was very unappealing. Almost without thinking she found herself wandering towards Halfway House, even though she knew it would probably not be open yet and no one else would be there anyway.

A car was parked outside the club, with two wheels on the pavement and the boot open. Sue was unloading cases of fizzy drinks into the front entrance.

'Hallo Evie, out from school early today? Haven't seen you for a bit. Go on in and I'll be there in a sec. Just got to move the car somewhere where it won't get booked. Ben's in the back room fiddling with the computers.'

Evie went into the club. It was eerily quiet when no one else was there, only one or two lights on, the CD player silent and the pool table empty of balls. The only sound came from the printer in the next room where Ben was working. She sat on a bar stool and waited for Sue.

'There we are. All sorted,' said Sue returning a moment later. She ripped a box open and began to unpack it, stacking the cans in rows in the fridge. 'So how's Evie these days? How're things going for the song contest? You and

Adam ready with the winning number? And what about the great romance?'

Evie winced.

'Oh dear, I'm sensing problems. Song contest or romance?'

'Both.'

'And...?'

Evie paused before replying. She wasn't sure how much she could tell Sue. But then, whatever bits she did tell would lead to other bits and in the end it was all mixed up together, so she might as well get the whole thing off her chest. Where to begin?

'Adam's gay,' she said flatly. It was the second time she'd said it that week but the words still sounded strange.

Sue sliced open another box, her expression of friendly interest never faltering for a second. 'How do you know?'

'He told me. It seems everyone in the whole world knew except me. Did you know?'

'Not exactly. I had an idea...'

'All this time, he's been gay and I didn't know. I'm supposed to be his best friend. Don't you tell things like that to your best friend?'

'Not necessarily,' said Sue. 'Sometimes saying things makes them real, so it's easier not to say them and then maybe they won't be true.'

'Yes, well. It's real, all right. And you'll never guess who it is he likes.' Might as well tell her everything.

'I don't know, but I'm kind of speculating it might be Dave?'

'Right again.'

'And how do you feel about that? Oh dear, sorry, I sound like Trisha off the telly. But you know what I mean.'

'How'm I supposed to feel? I don't even know whether it's wrong to be gay. I know what the vicar said in that talk he gave last term, but that was general, not about an actual person everybody knows. It feels quite different when it's your friend. Anyway,' Evie added, 'don't they say different things in different churches?'

Sue sighed. 'They do indeed.'

'So what am I supposed to think? Is it wrong for Adam to be gay? Should he be trying to get help to get over it? Why is he like that?'

Sue stopped unloading cans and sat down on a stool next to her. Her forehead wrinkled with concentration as she struggled to find the right words. 'Evie, maybe you're coming at it from the wrong direction.'

'What do you mean?'

'Well, all these questions you're asking focus on what's wrong, rather than what's right. That's quite a negative way of looking at things.'

'Yes, but doesn't the Bible say—?'

'The Bible says a lot of things. It doesn't say anything at all about it being wrong to have feelings for the same sex. We can't help the way we are. Yes, it does say things against two people of the same sex actually *having* sex, very strong things in some places, but you have to read it in the context in which it was written and remember who the writers were speaking to at the time. Some of what's in the Bible might be expressed rather differently if it was being written today.'

'But do you mean to say that what was wrong then is OK now? How can we ever be sure about anything if that's the case?'

'No, that's not what I'm saying at all. What I'm saying is that it's more helpful to look at the positive guidelines rather than make ourselves a list of "thou shalt nots".'

'I don't understand.'

'Well, if you want to see God's original plan for the human race you have to go right back to the beginning and creation.'

'Don't tell me, Adam and Eve. But surely that's not really true. Science has disproved it all. Evolution and all that.'

'That's a whole different issue; let's not get bogged down with that. The main point of the Adam and Eve story is that it's teaching us big truths about who we are and what our place is in the universe. Whether it actually happened or not is really pretty irrelevant. One of the reasons it's in the Bible is so that we can have a better understanding of why we are the way we are.'

'Yes, but what's that got to do with Adam? My Adam, I mean?'

'If you read the creation story you'll see that God made a good world. First of all, the actual world we live in, with the sun and the stars and the sea and all the animals and things that make it so beautiful. Then he made a man, a real live human being, and we're told he was good too, just like all the rest of creation.'

'Huh, something went badly wrong there, then,' muttered Evie.

Sue continued, 'And because God could see that people needed people or they'd get lonely, he gave the man a woman to keep him company. Then he told them to start a family. That's how it was right in the beginning, man, woman, children. Families. That was God's big plan and the way he thought people would thrive best. You won't find many people out there in the world who'll admit to agreeing with that idea, these days it's completely politically incorrect, but all the way through the Bible you see the pattern of men and women leaving their parents and setting up homes and having children. It's in the homes where the man and woman are faithful to each other and work to make the marriage last that children grow up secure and loved and valued and everyone becomes the person God means them to be.'

'Is this a private sermon or can anyone join in?' asked Ben who had come through from the computer room and was standing behind his wife.

'Not a sermon,' said Sue indignantly, 'I was just explaining to Evie—'

'I know, I've been listening from next door.'

'Anyway, the thing is,' Sue continued, ignoring him, 'it doesn't make any difference whether it's two blokes having sex, or two girls, or a boy and a girl; if it's a casual relationship with no commitment it's bound to be less than the best.'

Evie thought about Dave and how she'd nearly spent the night with him. That hadn't been casual on her part, but maybe it had been on his.

'But everybody does it,' she said. 'Like, *everybody*.'

'No, you're wrong, not everybody does it,' said Sue, 'although I agree it sometimes looks that way. But lots do, and look at the chaos it causes. Do you really think people are happy, going from one partner to another, never sure whether they're going to be discarded if someone better looking or more interesting comes along? As for what it does to children...'

'But thousands of families only have one parent,' objected Evie. 'Me and Adam for a start.'

'And don't you miss your mum?' put in Ben very gently. 'However great your dad is, aren't there times when you wish you could talk to someone with a female perspective on life?'

Evie let the question pass unanswered. 'So why did God make Adam - my Adam - this way?' she persisted. 'Did he make a mistake?'

'God doesn't make mistakes,' said Sue. 'At least, not as far as I can see. Every person he makes is different from the next and has the potential to be something quite remarkable. There are lots of reasons why some people are gay, sometimes to do with the way they've been brought up or the experiences they've had, but sometimes it just seems to be the way they are and there's no obvious reason.'

'Then does Adam need to be changed? To be cured or something?'

Ben laughed. 'Well, of course, in one way we all of us need to be changed. That's what growing as a Christian is all about. But not *cured*, any more than *you* could be cured of fancying fellas. What matters is how you handle those desires.'

'But you can't help it if you find someone, like, mega-attractive,' said Evie.

'Are we talking you or Adam here?' asked Ben.

'Either. Both.' She suddenly realised that she and Adam had been struggling with very similar problems.

''Course you can't help it,' said Sue. 'We all have feelings; we're all flesh and blood. That's what makes life so interesting. The real test is whether you decide to let those emotions rule your life rather than God. People say we live in a freer world than we used to, but it seems to me that if you always give in to the way you feel then you're not free at all. Your feelings have become your master.'

'But then you've got to be different all the time,' said Evie. 'Sounds like terribly hard work.'

'Even harder work to get yourself out of the mess you'll get into if you jump into bed with someone every time your hormones get a bit out of control.'

Evie was lost in thought for a few moments. 'I don't know how to help Adam,' she said at length. 'He's not going to listen to me. He thinks I'm just out to criticise him. It's 'cause of Tom, you see,' she explained.

'What's Tom got to do with anything?'

'He called Adam a poof and a pervert and all sorts of other awful things. Adam thinks I think the same way. He won't talk to me at all at the moment.'

'How much does his mum know?' asked Ben.

'Don't know.' Evie had wondered about that. It seemed unlikely that his mum could live in the same house as Adam and not realise what was going on in his head. But then she, Evie, hadn't known, so maybe it was possible that Julie was completely in the dark as well.

'I think maybe I'd better have a talk with Adam,' said Ben. 'Do you think that would help?'

'Anything would be better than the way things are at the moment. Apart from anything else, I can't sing in the final round of the contest if he doesn't finish my song.' She thought fleetingly about bringing up the subject of her dad and Julie, but the school day had come to an end and people were beginning to trickle into the club.

'OK, leave it with me. I'll see what I can do. Maybe I should talk to Tom too, if he'll let me. Sounds as though he needs to sort a few things out.'

Sue stood up and cleared the few remaining cans into the fridge. She said, 'We haven't really discussed you and Dave. Are you still seeing him?'

'No,' said Evie shortly.

'Understandable. But he must be wondering why you've dropped him so suddenly.'

'It's a bit more complicated than that,' said Evie, for the hundredth time revisiting the sight of Dave and Jade walking arm in arm up the hill. The memory was still like a punch in the stomach.

There was no time to elaborate. Vicki had arrived and was trying to catch her attention. The rest of the conversation would have to wait until later.

***

She arrived home to find two large vans outside her house, one labelled *J Thompson, Plumbing Installations and Repairs*, and the other marked *Sparky the Electrician. Flying to your Rescue*. Her dad was in the front hall wearing a sopping wet pair of trousers and an expression of extreme distress.

'What happened?'

'It's a long story. You know the toilet wouldn't flush properly? I decided there was something wrong with the pipe work so I was just trying to get at where it goes behind the bathroom wall. I could get to part of it but the rest was sealed in behind the basin and I couldn't reach it. So I got the drill out to go through the plasterboard—'

'—and drilled through an electric cable,' Evie finished for him.

'How did you know?' said her father in astonishment.

'Psychic.'

'Good gracious,' he said peering at her closely over his glasses, 'surely not? Anyway, everything went off with this huge bang, and then I realised I'd hit the pipe as well because there was water pouring out everywhere. Even then I thought I could probably manage to contain it all until I saw the pipe behind the bath was leaking too. And the wiring was getting all wet, so I thought I'd better get the professionals in.' Humiliation was written all over his face.

'Oh, Dad.' She hugged him. 'Never mind. It's not the end of the world, getting in the experts. Any more than it is when people call you in to help with their computers.'

'I know. I just thought I could handle it, and it's so annoying to have to pay someone.' He squeezed some water out of one the turn-ups on his trousers. 'Besides which, we have no electricity to cook a meal. How would you feel about a takeaway?'

'You know me. Takeaways are my favourite. Not that I don't think you're a brilliant cook,' she added hastily, catching the crestfallen look on his face.

'Shall we walk down to the Chinese? It's a lovely evening.'

'Yeah, but you'd better change your trousers.'

'Nah. Shan't bother. They'll dry off in the fresh air.'

Evie's dad donned his ancient khaki anorak with the tartan-lined hood and they ambled along the pavement in the dying sun, stopping from time to time to look at the more interesting front gardens. It was almost like the old times when her mum had been alive and the three of them used to take old Mrs Jenkins' dog out for evening walks, giving marks out of ten to people's lawns and flowerbeds. They had always awarded the highest scores to the grass with the straightest stripes, the most colourful borders and the most original garden ornaments, with points deducted for weeds.

This evening there was blossom everywhere, even in the bleakest corners where for the rest of the year nothing but scrubby bushes grew.

'If only it was always this nice,' sighed Evie, breathing in the sharp air. There was still enough of a sting in it to take away any illusions about summer having arrived.

George looked at her. 'You've been having a bad time, I think.'

'Mm,' she said distractedly. Then, 'Dad, can I ask you something?'

'Yep, sure. All ears. Fire away.'

'It's about Julie.'

His expression changed and a guarded look came over his face. 'What about Julie?'

'Are you and she... Are you seeing each other?'

'What a question. We see each other all the time, you know that,' he said evasively.

'You know what I mean. Are you Seeing each other with a capital S? As in going out? Because on the day when we came back from Llanwellyn, you remember? I saw the two of you walking along holding hands and looking all lovey-dovey. And you gave her a kiss.'

George looked very taken aback for a moment, then he grinned sheepishly and said, 'Curses. Rumbled.'

'You mean you are.' Evie took a moment to digest this information, then asked severely, 'Just how long has this been going on?'

'Come off it, Eves, I'm not a spotty teenager,' laughed her father. 'It's been "going on", as you call it, for a little while now.'

'How long is a little while? One year? Two years? Longer?'

'Don't be silly, two years ago your mum...' He stopped. 'Oh, Evie. You didn't think...?'

'Course I didn't,' she said quickly, overcome with confusion. She had never seen him look so shocked.

'But you did. You did. You really thought Julie and I were seeing each other while Mum was still alive. How could you?'

'I wasn't sure. How could I know? You kept going round there and mending things, even before Mum died. And you obviously liked being with her.'

'Why on earth wouldn't I? She's always been one of our closest friends. Evie, what on earth put such a dreadful idea in your head?'

'I can't explain. It's just something I had to know. I mean the thing is, if you're, you know, kind of going out with her now, that must mean you think she's nice to look at.'

'Indeed I do. She's a very attractive woman. Always has been.'

'But didn't you think so when you were round there mending things? When you were married to Mum?'

'Well, yes I did.'

'So weren't you even tempted to have an affair with her or something? How could you find her attractive and still love Mum?'

They'd arrived at the Chinese takeaway, so the conversation had to go on hold. Two boys from Evie's school were waiting at the counter and looked at them curiously as they went in. Her dad started to say something but she gave him a sharp nudge. 'Wait till we're outside again. Just order the food.'

'I was only going to ask if you wanted fried rice or plain boiled,' he said mildly. His glasses had misted up in the steamy atmosphere and one of the boys was staring at the damp patches on his trousers with added interest. Evie wished fervently, not for the first time, that he would buy a new coat.

They waited patiently while the Chinese girl behind the counter wrapped portions of beef and cashew, sweet-and-sour pork and spare ribs. George paid for them and passed Evie a big bag of prawn crackers. 'Don't eat them all before we get home,' he warned.

It felt quite cold outside again after the warmth of the shop. The sun was getting low and Evie shivered as she waited for her dad to answer her question.

He took some time to speak. Then he said, 'Your mum was the most important person in the whole world to me. No one will ever take her place. I don't think anyone will ever know what it felt like when she died. I loved her to bits. You know that really, don't you?'

Evie nodded. She did know.

'When I married her I promised before God to love her for better for worse, richer or poorer, sickness and health, all that stuff you say at the wedding service. And I certainly got the sickness and health bit.' He reached over and stole a prawn cracker from Evie's paper bag. 'Loving someone for a whole lifetime is something you make a conscious decision to do. Love isn't just a feeling, although it's certainly that. It's also a choice. I could have chosen to give up when things got difficult, I could even have chosen to go off with Julie when your mum's hair started falling out and she was always tired and couldn't do much.'

'That would have been an *awful* thing to do!'

'Of course it would, and that's why I didn't do it. In fact, it never even occurred to me, and Julie wouldn't have contemplated it either. But being married doesn't stop you from finding other people attractive. It's what you do with that attraction that counts. Just imagine what Mum's last months would have been like if I'd abandoned her when she needed me most.'

'So did you never stop loving Mum?'

'Absolutely not. I loved her to the very last day and I still love her. Whatever happens between me and Julie now will never change that.' He munched on another prawn cracker. 'Would you be so upset if Julie and I got closer? You and Adam being such good friends and all?'

'Not at the moment, we're not,' said Evie gloomily.

She poured out the last week's happenings to her dad, carefully omitting to mention her intention to deceive him and go to Dave's house. George let her talk, occasionally asking questions, but mostly listening quietly.

By the time she'd finished they were home. Both the vans had left and the electricity was back on.

'Funny how much you take light for granted,' said George, illuminating the kitchen with a flick of a switch. He spread out the food on the table and they settled down to eat. 'Poor old Adam. He must be in a real muddle. Julie suspected something like this. I wonder if he really is gay,' he ruminated.

'Haven't you been listening to a word I've been saying?' said Evie in exasperation. Sometimes her dad could be really thick.

'Yes, sure I have, but some people think they're gay in their teens and then grow out of it as they get older. I had quite a crush on a senior boy when I was school. But then it was an all-boys school and I didn't get to meet any girls till I was quite grown-up.'

Evie choked explosively on a piece of pork. 'Dad. Perlease. Don't be obscene.'

'It does happen. But from what you say, I don't think Adam is in that category. Well, difficult times ahead for him. He's going to need all the friends he can get. Lucky he's got you.'

'I don't think he wants me right now.'

'He'll get over it. You say Ben's going to have a chat with him? Perhaps that'll help.'

Evie picked up a spare rib in her fingers and chewed on it. Lurid red sauce trickled down her sleeve and George passed her a grubby tissue. She smiled at him as she dabbed at her school blouse.

She felt more light-hearted than she had for weeks. She'd never have thought he would be so easy to talk to. Funny mixture, her dad. He could be surprisingly understanding at times. If you ignored the computer obsession and the DIY, and the anorak of course, there were moments when he seemed quite normal. Wise, even.

Ten

The Easter holidays had begun. Evie's dad had a huge backlog of work to get through and could only afford to take off the long Bank Holiday weekend in the middle, so for most of the time Evie was left alone in the bungalow. She had vague plans to revise for her GCSEs, but when it came to it she found it almost impossible to settle down to work. The exams still seemed a long way in the future, and anyway it was very difficult to concentrate when there was so much stuff churning around her brain. During the first week she got up very late every day and mooched around the house, every so often pausing to flick though the TV channels or to raid the fridge or fruit bowl for provisions when the pangs of hunger got too great. In the afternoons she wandered into town to window-shop, knowing she would almost certainly meet school friends doing the same thing.

Halfway House was open in the afternoons. There was a table tennis tournament going on during the holidays, but she only looked in once or twice, still nervous about who she might see. Most of the usual helpers were away for the first few days and the club was run by people she didn't know very well. But in the second week, the day after the Bank Holiday Monday, Sue was back behind the bar. Her two youngest children, six-year-old twins with dark curly hair and huge brown eyes, were sitting at the counter drawing pictures.

'Hallo stranger,' she greeted Evie. 'Where've you been? Saw you in the distance in church on Easter Day, but didn't get a chance to chat. I've been hoping to catch up with you. Thought you'd want to know Ben's been up to see Adam this week. He spent some time with Tom too, and their mum.'

'And?'

'They had a good talk and I think Adam's going to have a chat with someone who's a bit more experienced than Ben in this sort of thing. Hasn't he phoned you?'

'No.'

'Well, don't worry, I'm sure he will. Just give him time to sort himself out a bit. That's a beautiful car you've drawn, Joey,' she added to her son. 'What colour are you going to do it?'

'And my submarine! Look at my lovely submarine! 'S'better than Joey's old car!' clamoured her daughter, holding up her piece of paper for approval.

'Yes, yours is lovely too,' agreed her mother, 'they're both really special. Sorry, Evie, difficult to concentrate with the kids around during the holidays. What are you doing with your time off?'

'Work,' said Evie vaguely.

It was sort of true. She'd made an excellent revision timetable that very morning, devoting different days to different subjects right up to half-term. Each subject had been allocated a colour so that it was easy to see which exam she was revising for on any particular day, and for this last bit of the holidays (four days), she'd done special spaces highlighted in yellow to denote breaks for drinks, breaks for lunch and breaks for *Neighbours*. It would all be highly efficient if only she could get up in the morning in time to start working before the first drinks break.

Anyway, when she'd taken a quick survey among her friends in the club she'd found that hardly any of them had even got as far as a timetable, let alone any revision, so she could afford to feel a little smug. That was why she didn't really think it mattered that she'd spent half her holidays watching daytime TV.

This morning she'd been flicking through the channels and had come across a chat show on the theme 'My son/daughter is gay.' Evie watched it with interest, curious to see what people would have to say. Parental reactions seemed to cover a whole range from warm approval to disgusted outrage; somehow neither seemed to be exactly appropriate. Once again she wondered how Julie would be handling what was now common knowledge about Adam.

She hadn't really discussed it with her father any more; the chilled-out mood that had existed on their walk to the Chinese takeaway seemed to have evaporated slightly, and some of the old barriers had come back. The thing about adults, she reflected, was that sometimes you wanted to talk to them, but at other times it was just painfully embarrassing. There was no way of knowing in advance when it was going to be OK; you just had to go with the flow.

***

The summer term had started before she saw Adam again, although summer was bit of a misnomer; minor hurricanes seemed to have struck Stanworth and all the blossom was blowing off the trees in a pale pink snowstorm.

She spotted him on the first day of term, hurrying through a gale towards the science block, hair sticking out at all angles from the force of the wind. He paused when she called his name and waited for her to catch up.

'Adam. I've missed you.'

He grinned awkwardly. 'I know. I'm sorry. I just...' he groped for the right words.

'Ad, you know I never meant...' started Evie.

'I didn't really...' he said at exactly the same moment. Simultaneously they stopped.

'There isn't time now,' he said. 'I'll come over to your house.'

She nodded, the wind whipping her hair against her neck. 'Soon?'

'Tomorrow. Not tonight, have something I must do. Can't stop now, late for biology. I will come, honest, straight after tea. Half seven?'

She would have to be content with that. He was already striding off down the concrete path, dodging broken twigs as he walked. Suddenly he stopped again, turned back and shouted something, but a gust of air snatched his words away.

'What?' yelled Evie.

He was mouthing again. She just caught the words '...best song ever...' He waited there for a second, obviously not sure if she had heard, then shrugged his shoulders and carried on round the corner of the science labs.

***

By late evening the winds had reached a ferocious intensity. Even Evie, who didn't usually pay much attention to the weather, was impressed by the sound of the squalls whistling round the house. Her father fretted around, muttering about his new plants and the state of the roof tiles.

Evie looked in to the living room to say goodnight on her way to bed and found him flipping anxiously through the regional reports on Ceefax.

'Think we might just catch the forecast on BBC,' he said, patting the cushion beside him. She perched on the arm of the sofa, watching over his shoulder as the weather girl waved her hand at the black clouds on the map behind her.

'Bad news,' said her dad, shaking his head dolefully at the 'Severe Weather Warning' appearing on a red band across the bottom of the screen. 'It's destructive enough when the wind blows up like this in late autumn, but at least nearly all the leaves are off the trees by then. At this time of year, when everything's coming out and the branches are so heavy, the damage can be immense.' He pressed the off-button on the TV controls, picked up his newspaper and stood up. 'Put the lights out, would you?'

Tired from the long day at school, Evie fell asleep almost immediately, in spite of the sound of the wind roaring round the bungalow, the persistent tapping noise from a hanging branch by her window and the insistent patter of raindrops.

Suddenly there was a loud bang on the roof. She sat bolt upright, instantly wide awake, wondering what could have caused the crash. She jumped out of bed and, following the direction of the sound, went out into the hall to peer out of the window. Her dad was already there, dressing gown over his blue checked pyjamas and torch in hand.

'I'm going out to look,' he said. As he opened the front door a great blast of air swept though the bungalow.

He was back in less than a minute. 'TV aerial. The whole thing's come down off the roof. Look, you can see part of it on the grass there.' A long metal rod lay on the patch of front garden, surrounded by bits of blossom and rubbish which had blown off the road over the fence. 'No telly for you tomorrow,' said her father.

Evie padded back to bed, snuggled into the warmth of her duvet and lay listening to the gale raging round outside.

P'raps God's trying to say something to me, she thought ruefully, remembering all the daytime TV she'd watched over the holidays when she should have been revising. Seemed a bit of a drastic measure, smiting the aerial like that, but then you could never tell with God.

***

The winds raged on well into the next day, but by early afternoon the noise had dropped to a gentler background drone. The last period of the day was French, and Evie arrived in the classroom to find that the only free place was at a table next to Jade. There was no escape. Evie laid her books on the floor and slid into the chair beside her just as the lesson was beginning.

Without a flicker of expression Jade tore a piece of paper out of her rough book, scrawled the words *Must talk* in small loopy writing and passed it to her. Evie glanced at it, wrote *What about?* and handed it back.

Dave wrote Jade.

Oh yes, your boyfriend scribbled Evie in big angry letters.

Miss Porter was looking at them suspiciously. They both sat very still for a few moments.

Jade picked up her pen again. *Not my boyfriend.*

Well certainly not mine wrote Evie.

Miss Porter was talking about verbs that went with *avoir*. Jade fixed her with a stare of intense interest and without looking down at the page inscribed *Didn't stay with him that Saturday.*

Evie let out a barely suppressed snort of disbelief.

'Yes, Evie?' said Miss Porter. 'You'd like to tell us some past participles which go with *avoir*?'

'Um, sure,' said Evie, wildly racking her brain for some long forgotten scrap of information. 'How about um, *aller? J'ai allé.*'

'Meaning...?' said Miss Porter. Her voice was dangerously quiet.

'I went?' said Evie uncertainly. A few of the class tittered.

'Oh dear, dear,' said Miss Porter in mock horror. '*Quel horreur! Avoir* and *aller*. What a terrible mistake. I thought

128

we went over all this at the end of last term. Someone tell Eve what verb we use with *aller*.'

One of the boys near the front shot his hand into the air. '*Etre*, Miss Porter.'

'Exactly. *Etre. Je suis allée*. I think Eve and Jade have been thinking about something else. Do you want to share what's in your exercise book with the class, Jade?'

'No, Miss Porter.'

'Well then, kindly concentrate for the rest of the lesson. Someone tell these two poor girls a verb you could use with *avoir*.'

'*Aimer*?' said the boy at the front. He hadn't even bothered to put his hand up this time.

'Excellent. *Aimer* is a good one. *J'ai aimé*. What does that mean, Eve?'

'I did love,' said Evie. 'Or maybe, I loved.' A ripple of laughter ran round the classroom.

'Touching. You did love. All in the past. Better luck next time, eh?'

'Yes, Miss Porter.'

Before long the pips went for the end of the day and Evie seized her school bag for a quick exit.

'Hey, wait,' said Jade, 'I thought we were going to talk?'

'No time,' said Evie. She was not in the mood for that particular conversation. Anyway, Adam was coming round and she needed to get tea and homework out of the way before he arrived.

By half-past seven she was ready for him, meal cleared away and homework done. She sat on the sofa in the living room, feet up in front of her on the coffee table, and idly leafed through a magazine.

Eight o'clock came and went. It was almost completely dark outside. The TV still wasn't working; apparently half the aerials in the neighbourhood had been put out of action the night before and it had been impossible for her dad to get anyone to repair theirs. Her magazine long finished, Evie started looking round for something to do.

Her father looked up from the crossword. 'Settle down, Evie. He'll be here in a moment. You know Adam; he gets caught up in other things and forgets the time. Give him a ring if you're worried.'

'Perhaps I will.' She went into the hall to find the phone but stopped in front of the porch.

A letter lay on the doormat, a long thin envelope with the single word 'Evie' scrawled across the middle. Instantly recognising Adam's handwriting, she opened the front door and peered out in both directions into the street, but there was no sign of anyone on the pavement.

She sat on the floor in the middle of the hall and began to read.

***

Dear Evie

I never wrote a letter to you before, it feels really weird. We've always just talked in the past, haven't we? I know we were meant to meet tonight but there's things I want to say to you and I don't think I can look you in the eye while I do it cos I don't really know what you might be thinking and I'm scared. When I saw you in school yesterday I guessed we must still be friends so I'm taking the risk of writing to explain things.

I'm sorry I never told you about what was going on with me. I know you must feel let down by that. It wasn't cos you're not my best friend, you are, but it was cos I thought it might be the end of that friendship. You saw how Tom was when he found out, I didn't want it to be the same with you.

I can't help the way I am. At the beginning I thought that it might go away, but the more I tried to ignore my feelings the worse they got. The really difficult thing has been worrying that I must be some sort of second-class citizen, that there's something wrong with me, that I'm different from everyone else. When we had that talk from the vicar last year I just wanted to run away and hide. It was like he was telling me I was a hopeless Christian and that God could never love me. I know that's not really what he said at all but that's how it felt.

Geoff at school says he's gay too and Melissa Knowles in the top year. It's no big deal for them because they don't believe in God and think that the way you live is your own business. I just don't find it that easy. But it wasn't till I met Dave that I realised I was going to have to face up to it all because the feelings I had for him were so strong. Still are, if I'm honest. (I hope this isn't shocking you.)

Anyway, Ben came to see me over the holidays and we had this long talk, very deep. He's great, Ben, you can just be yourself with him and not have to do any pretending. For the first time in ages I felt as though I was important to someone. I mean, I knew in my head that I was important to Mum and God and all that stuff, but it wasn't till I talked to Ben that I really realised it properly. The amazing thing was that that he made me feel that being gay contributed to the kind of person I am. Can you imagine that, Eves? It's as if it's part of what makes me Adam Kendall. And he said that what mattered was not that I had these feelings but what I chose to do with them. That's the bit I've got to work out next. We talked about what it would mean to live the kind of lifestyle a lot of gay people follow – going to places where similar people meet, like gay clubs and stuff – and how it devalues a person to keep going from one relationship to another, but if that's wrong, how am I going to cope with the way I am? What does God want me to do with my life?

Since Ben came round I've spent a whole lot of time thinking. I have this strange feeling that my life is only just beginning, that up till now I've just been staggering from one crisis to another with no power to do anything to help myself. Now it's all out in the open I have the weirdest feeling that God has all sorts of things planned for me and that what I have to do is find out what they are and do them. It's pretty exciting really, for the first time I feel really free.

You probably think I'm totally off my trolley, but I hope you'll try to understand. I wonder how you'll react to this letter?

The good news is I've finished your song! Think you'll like it. Come round soon and I'll play it to you.

> *Lots of love,*
> *Your good mate,*
> *Adam*

PS Is it my imagination or have your dad and my mum been behaving a bit strangely together lately?

Evie dropped the letter on the floor, reached for the phone and called his number.

***

The song was called 'All of me'. It had a bluesy flavour to it, the kind of thing you could croon, a sort of cross between Jamie Cullum and black soul music. Evie thought it was marvellous. She sat on the edge of an armchair in the Kendalls' living room and listened in silence, her toe tapping in time with the beat as Adam played it on his keyboard. The lyrics were different from anything he'd ever written before;

instead of being about unrequited love and despair they were full of hope and longing.

> *...And knowing all of me, you love me,*
> *Knowing all of me, you care.*
> *This time I'm gonna give you*
> *All of me.*

'Well, what d'you think?' he asked as the last notes faded away.

'It's brilliant. Really brilliant. I mean, the style might not appeal to everyone, but it's got such – such –' she searched for the right word, '– such *feeling*, you couldn't just listen and not be sucked in.'

He beamed. 'Do you think so?'

'I really do. Is it meant to be about someone you know or is it about God?'

'Either, really. I mean it could be someone just talking about an earthly person they love or that person could be God. I couldn't get the tune how I wanted it till a couple of days ago, then suddenly it all came right. I think maybe in my subconscious it's always been first and foremost about God.'

'Play it again so that I can learn it, then I'll have a go.'

He sang it through again, repeating the verses and the refrain so that she could pick up the melody, then she stood beside him and sang while he accompanied her on the keyboard. It was harder than it had seemed on first hearing, as the tune didn't always go where she expected and there were some long notes in the chorus that made her quite breathless.

'It's going to take some practice,' she said, after a while. 'I'll probably need to come round a few times till we get it right.'

'No worries,' said Adam. 'I'm not going anywhere.' He smiled and a wave of relief swept over Evie as she recognised signs of the return of their easy friendship. He was still the same old Adam, even though things were still a bit strange between them.

'Your letter—' she said.

'I know, I'm not very good at saying what I mean. But it was for real.'

'No, it was nice. No, nice is wrong, it was *truthful*.'

He fingered the keyboard thoughtfully and sounded a couple of notes. 'What about you and Dave? Are you over him?'

She dropped her gaze from his face. 'Not really. You?'

'No, me neither.' There was an awkward pause. What a bizarre conversation, thought Evie. I guess I was wrong. Things are never really going to go completely back to normal.

'Actually,' said Adam, appearing to summon up courage for the piece of news he had to impart, 'Dave's going away.'

'What do you mean, going away?'

'Tom told me. He's been offered a job in London. You know he applied to do that course at the PE college in Wimbledon? Marshall's, the firm he's been modelling sports gear for, have offered to sponsor him right through college in return for him working full-time for them over the summer. He'll get paid as well, jammy thing. So he'll be gone as soon as exams are over. Off to the Big Smoke. End of June at the latest.'

'Oh,' said Evie, forlornly. The world suddenly seemed a little emptier.

''S'gotta be good, Eves. Good for him and good for you and me. This way we all get to start again.'

'S'pose so,' said Evie uncertainly. She tried to imagine how things would be with Dave gone. 'It's not going to take away the problem, though, is it?'

'What problem?'

'You know, about the way you are...' She still didn't have the right words to talk about it.

'No, it won't go away. I guess I'll just have to face each situation as it arises.' For a moment he looked as if he was about to say more, then he seemed to think the better of it. He shrugged, and she regarded him with admiration.

'Does your mum know all about it?'

'Yes. She does now. She'd always suspected there was something different about me. After Tom and the way he goes on about girls it must look kinda obvious.'

'And is she cool with it?'

'I don't think cool is quite how I'd describe it. It must've been a shock even though she suspected. But she's great, my mum, always been my biggest fan and nothing'll change that. Her main worry is how it'll affect my friendships and stuff.'

'And Tom? Has he come round to the idea?'

Adam's face clouded over. 'Tom's a jerk,' he said briefly.

Evie quickly changed the subject. 'All right if I take this home with me to learn the words?' she asked, lifting the sheet of music from the keyboard.

'Course. That's the whole idea. I can easily print it off again.'

'You're dead clever, writing music on the computer,' she said, with respect. 'Thought my dad was the only person who could do that kind of thing.'

'Not just a pretty face.' Adam suddenly remembered something. 'Talking of your dad, what about him and my mum?'

She grinned at him and winked conspiratorially. 'The answer's yes. At least I think so.'

His mouth fell open. 'Not really.'

'Yep. First-hand info. Nothing at all official in sight yet, but it looks like Lurve with a great big capital L.'

'You're joshing me. I mean, I thought it looked that way, but then reckoned I had to be imagining it.'

'No, it's really true. A deep and meaningful relationship founded on a mutual love of income tax and the inner workings of your mum's tumble dryer.'

'Awesome. What could be a better foundation?' said Adam with delight. 'You'll have to do something about that anorak of his, though. My mum's got her street cred to keep up, she's well known round here for being a babe of age.'

'Do you mind, that's my dad you're slagging off? Waterproof polyester is the new leather, didn't you know?'

'Yeah, right. And slightly balding is the new Keanu Reeves haircut, I suppose?'

'Of course it is.'

'Of *course* it is.'

Eleven

Johnny Harker, lead singer of *Delusion*, drove a car which was not quite a stretch limo but which was definitely going that way. It was long and sleek and black and the dashboard sported a space-age sound system that looked more like Mission Control at NASA than a device for playing CDs. He liked to drive the car with all the windows wound down and the noise turned up and consequently, as he manoeuvred the machine into his reserved space in front of the main door of the Town Hall, the sound of the heavy beat from his stereo could be heard two or three streets away in every direction.

A small crowd had gathered at the entrance to see him arrive for the final of the song competition. They were rewarded by the sight of a young man in his mid-twenties with dark tousled hair emerging from the car. He was dressed in a charcoal shirt and cream-coloured trousers with a matching jacket flung casually over one shoulder. There was a small round of applause and someone shouted, 'Hallo, Johnny!' He waved at the waiting group and disappeared into the building.

Inside he was scooped up by Ben who had been waiting for him in the foyer with the other judges. They were all there, the music teachers armed with their notepads and pens, Shelley encased in a flimsy silver tube-like garment and Vernon Eastwood in his familiar black T-shirt and eyepatch.

'Can you credit the nerve of the man?' said Evie to Vicki, watching them come into the main hall. 'No one believes the glass eye story any more, yet he still wears that thing.'

The two girls had been banished with the other three finalists to a meeting room for the whole competition but they could get a reasonable view of both the judges and the audience through a crack in the double doors. There was too much noise and Johnny Harker was too far away for them to be able to hear what he was saying, but he had clearly got to work on Shelley, holding her hand for much longer than was necessary after shaking it, and gazing down at her with undisguised admiration. He must be more than a foot taller than her, Evie reckoned.

Evie had never felt so nervous before in her whole life. The hall was completely full with swarms of people from Greenlands, Stanworth High and the Sixth Form College, and a good number from St Michael's as well. Several parents had put in an appearance, including George and Julie who were sitting next to each other near the front. Adam, who was to accompany her live on the keyboard, was there in the changing room, giving her last minute advice.

'Now, don't forget, Eves,' he said, 'quietly for the first verse, then getting louder, then quiet again in the bit where you sing the chorus for the third time. Then a really big ending.'

Evie nodded, they had rehearsed it over and over again. Even so, she was terrified. She had a sneaking suspicion that the song was too big for her, the notes went so high and she had to hold them for so long. Most of all she was scared she would let Adam down.

There was a lull in the sound of excited chatter and Ben was on stage, speaking to the audience.

'Good evening, everyone, and a warm welcome to Stanworth's answer to *Pop Idol*, our first ever inter-school singing contest. It's great to see so many faces, familiar and unfamiliar, in the Town Hall for this very special occasion.'

He beamed round the hall. 'Welcome too, to our panel of expert judges, most of them known to you in one way or another. And an extra special welcome to Stanworth's very own Johnny Harker, familiar to all of you, I'm sure, as the lead singer of *Delusion*, a band which has reached the number one slot in the charts no less than three times.' Johnny waved at the audience and was rewarded with cheers and catcalls. Several of the audience stamped their feet noisily and Ben had to wait a few moments for the noise to die down.

'Each of the contestants you will see tonight has had to beat off stiff competition to be here. This is the third round and in each round the number of contestants has been narrowed down. The second round was particularly fruitful – ' he paused briefly as a good-natured groan ran round the hall, '– and I'm sure the judges will agree that the decision to reduce the list down to these five finalists was reached with great difficulty.' The two music teachers nodded vigorously. Vernon Eastwood sat impassively, while Shelley whispered something to Johnny Harker, who smiled.

Ben continued, 'So first of all it is my great pleasure to ask Martin Fraser to come forward and sing for us. Martin goes to Stanworth Sixth Form College and has brought his own backing band here tonight. He's chosen to sing a Randall Cooper song entitled "Bemused". Ladies and gentlemen, Martin Fraser!'

Martin pushed past Evie through the door, and to the sound of enthusiastic applause made his way out to the steps leading up to the stage.

'He looks as nervous as I feel,' observed Vicki. She peered into the mirror to check her make-up. 'Can you lend me some blusher, Eves?' She was wearing a light turquoise halter neck dress and looked completely dazzling.

'In my bag,' said Evie, without taking her eyes off the stage. Martin was good, very good, but she didn't think his song was as strong as hers. All of the competitors had abandoned recorded tapes and were using live accompaniment in this round. Martin was backed by a small group from the Sixth Form College consisting of two guitars and drums.

Ben had decided against them performing in alphabetical order this time so that the girls wouldn't be left to the end, but even so Evie found to her annoyance that she was to be last once again.

'When I get married, I'm going to make quite sure it's to someone with a surname beginning with A,' she told Adam. 'Two As would be best, like Aaron. Or at the very least AB, like Abercrombie or Abbot.'

The name Abbot made her think of Jade. Evie craned her neck to see if she was in the audience. There she was, quite near the back, wedged between Brooksie and a girl from their school.

Martin had finished and the judges were speaking.

'Shut up and listen,' said Paul from the corner. He was sitting on a low stool, guitar on his lap, biting the nails on his right hand and fingering silent chords with his left.

The judges had lots to say about Martin, nearly all complimentary. Most of it was wasted on Evie, who was helping Vicki with final touches to her make-up, but Adam listened intently.

'How did he do?' Evie asked, wiping a smudge of mascara from the corner of Vicki's eye.

'They said he was too quiet. It sounds different in here compared with Halfway House, it's much bigger. You're going to have to sing really loudly.'

'If I can get any sound out at all. I dreamed last night it was the final, and the more I opened my mouth, the more nothing happened.'

Vicki was ready now. 'How do I look? Is my hair OK?' She patted the top of her head.

'Stunning. Get out there and show 'em, girl.'

Vicki had chosen a song that was bang up to date, currently number eight in the charts. Like Evie she had a keyboard accompaniment and besides that there was a boy from her school playing a saxophone during the instrumental bits. The effect was electric.

'You realise we haven't a hope,' said Evie gloomily to Adam as they propped themselves against the door, watching Vicki's act.

'Don't be such a wuss,' he replied. 'Just believe in yourself for once. OK, they're both good, but you're good too.'

Hannah, who had been waiting quietly until now, piped up, 'Yes, but Johnny Harker's bound to go for Vicki or Paul, 'cause they both go to his old school.'

'Which he hated,' put in Paul from his corner. He was tightening the strings on his guitar, pausing every so often to pluck one and listen closely to the pitch.

'How do you know?' said Adam.

'Everyone knows. He left early. Expelled. Drugs-related, I think. Something people conveniently forget when they want him to come back here and do the returning hero bit.'

'I wonder why he comes back, then, 'said Evie.

'Family ties. He still goes to see his mum. It's not all glitz and glamour at the top, you know, people are what matter at the end of the day.'

'But here he is, trying to help someone else into the showbiz world,' said Evie. 'He must think it's worth doing.'

'Probably the money,' said Hannah.

'Might be for him. But you have to remember that for every Johnny Harker who makes it to the big time there are a squillion hopefuls like you and me who never make it beyond Stanworth Town Hall. Even Johnny will only be at the top for a short time, and then what?'

'It's gotta be worth a try, though, if you've got talent, hasn't it?' said Adam. He eyed himself in the mirror. 'Do you think my hair should stick up at the front or lie flat?'

Vicki's song had finished and very gingerly she stepped down from the stage, taking great care not to trip on the stairs. Safely back in the side room with the remaining competitors, she kicked her shoes off and collapsed into one of the plastic stacking chairs that lined the wall.

'That was *hideous*! Did you see Vernon Eastwood? He just stared at my knees the whole time as if he was trying to work out what the knocking sound was. And Johnny Harker was talking to Shelley all the way through! He can't have heard a word I was singing. I was so-o awful.'

'Rubbish, you were great, Vick,' said Evie, with conviction. 'I'll be happy if I'm half that good.'

Hannah's name was being called. She took a deep breath and stepped out into the hall, blinking in the glare of the lights as she walked up to the stage.

Her performance was mildly disappointing. In previous rounds she had held the microphone easily and sung with confidence, but in front of this audience her movements seemed wooden and jerky. Probably just the effect of nerves, thought Evie, determining not to fall in the same trap when her turn came. The judges seemed to have a similar opinion, which gave Evie some encouragement although she was ashamed of herself for such uncharitable feelings. For the first time that evening she began to relax a little.

Paul was next. He had kept very quiet about what he was going to sing, and now the reason for his secrecy became evident. He had chosen a *Delusion* song, a song that had actually been written by Johnny Harker, a gentle compelling ballad about a lost love.

'What a nerve!' exclaimed Evie, recognising the opening lines. 'How could anyone possibly think Johnny would prefer Paul's version to his own?'

But Adam was chuckling quietly to himself. 'It is quite a risk. But it's a compliment too, when you come to think about it. Perhaps Johnny will be so flattered by how good it sounds that he'll give all his marks to Paul. And I'm sure the fact he's doing his own accompaniment will be in his favour.'

The audience clearly liked it. They clapped and whistled and called loudly for encores so that eventually Ben had to go up on stage to calm them down before the judges' voices could be heard.

'Great singing,' said Vernon Eastwood. 'Each round better then the last. You should go far.'

'A lovely relaxed manner,' said Shelley. 'You're a joy to listen to.'

'Beautiful chord modulations,' added Mr Barraclough.

'Although not what was originally written,' interjected Johnny Harker with some spirit. 'I think you've messed about with my tune, haven't you?'

'Not the tune,' said Paul nervously, 'just the chord progressions. I just thought for my voice—'

'Quite right,' agreed Johnny robustly. 'Your voice is quite different from mine. I liked the way you adapted it to fit. It's a great song, though I say it myself, and I reckon you've done it justice. Nice work, man.'

And now it was Evie's turn.

Her hands were so damp with sweat she thought the droplets must be visible from the back of the hall. She emerged from the side room and began the long journey to the short flight of stairs leading up to the stage.

'We can do it, Eves,' whispered Adam, close behind her. The narrow side aisle between her and the platform stretched out endlessly so that Ben seemed about a million miles away as he beckoned her up, smiling encouragingly and lowering his head to speak into the microphone.

'... And a big welcome for Eve Wilson and *"All of Me"*!'

Her knees shook as she climbed the steps. Somewhere in the distance she could see George and Julie smiling broadly at her but the audience looked very far away, cut off by the row of judges at the front.

Adam stood at the keyboard and played the introduction. Over the last couple of weeks the song had become part of her, she knew it so well. But here, in this big hall, with all these people watching she felt as if it was completely new, as though she was trying it out for the first time. She opened her mouth and for a frightening second nothing came out. Then she began to sing.

At once the melody took hold of her and she poured her soul into it, all the time remembering snippets of advice Adam had given her. *Quietly now, hold that note, now cut it off.* The hall was silent, the whole audience focused on her. Mr Barraclough was scribbling on the pad in front of him, Vernon Eastwood was sitting watching her with his arms folded, apparently transfixed.

Build up now, but don't get any faster, Adam's words went through her head. *And now for the big ending, hands in the air, head held high.*

> *This time I'm gonna give you*
> *All - of - me!*

There was a second's silence then a burst of rapturous applause. Evie turned to Adam, her eyes shining.

'I think they liked it,' she said.

The applause died down and one by one the judges spoke.

'What a great song,' said the Greenlands music teacher. 'Where did you get it from, dear?'

'My friend, Adam, wrote it,' said Evie, wondering why her voice suddenly sounded so small.

'Use the mike,' whispered Adam.

'My friend, Adam, wrote it,' she repeated into the microphone, loud and clear.

'You're the young lady who did the same song as someone else last time, aren't you?' said Vernon Eastwood. 'Well, my advice is stick with Adam all the way; I don't think he'll let you down. You were excellent.'

'I love your trousers,' added Shelley. 'Different shoes, perhaps?'

Evie looked down at her feet. She was particularly fond of her purple sandals.

Johnny Harker leaned back in his chair and chewed the end of his pencil. 'I agree, it was a great song, no doubt about that, but I wasn't sure you did it justice. That last note, for instance. It would have been more effective if you'd held it on longer.'

Evie said nothing. She'd nearly burst her lungs hanging on to that note.

'And a couple of times, it may have been my imagination, but I got the impression you were a bit out of tune.'

'I think that's unfair,' interrupted Mr Barraclough. 'Eve sings very well in tune. I think you only got that impression because she was nervous.'

'Ah yes, but there's no room for nerves with a true professional,' said Johnny. 'I realise I'm just nit-picking here, but we're looking for perfection. Right, Ben?'

'I think it's time for the judges to come to their final decision,' said Ben smoothly. 'We'll give you ten minutes in the back meeting room and then ask you to come through and give your verdict.'

The five judges rose to their feet and trooped out behind the stage.

Instantly the hall began to buzz with heated conversations as everyone put forward their opinions as to who the winner should be. Evie and Adam descended from the stage and went over to join their parents.

'You were fantastic,' said Julie, giving Evie a hug. 'Easily the best. I'm dead proud of you both.'

'I never knew you could sing like that,' said her father. 'Just like your mum.'

'I can't. It was the song that did it,' said Evie.

'As for that nonsense about your shoes! Who does that Shelley person think she is?' said Julie. 'Fine one she is to talk, wearing nothing but a leg warmer.'

Over twenty minutes passed before the judges finally emerged. Mr Barraclough passed Ben an envelope and they all returned to their seats. Ben went up on to the platform once more and took the microphone. An expectant hush descended on the hall.

'I feel just like someone awarding the Oscars,' he smiled, as he ripped open the envelope. He pulled out a piece of paper and scanned it briefly before looking up and addressing the audience.

'Well, ladies and gentlemen, it's been a wonderful evening. I think you'll agree the quality of songs has been very high.'

'Come *on*,' fidgeted Evie.

'The judges have found it extremely difficult to make up their minds but they have now come to a decision which I'm going to read out to you. Ladies and gentlemen, in reverse order, the winners are...' he paused and looked around.

'In third place, Vicki Stilwell with *"Coming Home"*.'

Vicki smiled bravely as the audience clapped and whistled. Evie reached over and squeezed her arm in an effort to convey congratulations and sympathy all at once.

'In second place, and I want to repeat, this was a very tough decision for the judges...'

'I'll give him tough decision,' muttered Adam.

'... in second place, Evie Wilson with *"All of me"*.'

A huge cheer erupted from the Greenlands contingent as they realised what was coming next.

'And the winner, ladies and gentlemen, of Stanworth's first inter-school singing contest, with a classic performance of Johnny Harker's *"Street Fantasy"*, is Paul Davidson. Would you like to come up here and collect your prize, Paul?'

***

Evie sat at the back of the hall and waited for Adam to pack up his keyboard. She was sitting on a grubby stone step at the bottom of a flight of stairs that led up to the gallery, tucked away at the rear end of the building. Most of the audience had already dispersed, George and Julie with them. The contest had gone on for nearly another hour after the announcement of the winner, with photographs for the local newspapers, a speech by Johnny Harker and then Paul performing his winning song again. The atmosphere in the hall had been cheerfully tolerant; both Greenlands and Stanworth High applauding the winner with equal enthusiasm, their previous rivalries forgotten.

All of which did nothing to lessen the huge sense of disappointment that overwhelmed Evie as she relived the last couple of hours. In fact, it wasn't until the judges had come to their final verdict that she realised just how badly she had wanted to be first. She'd been so sure her song was a winner, not just because it was good, but because she'd spent so long learning it and rehearsing her whole act. To get so far and then to be pipped at the final post! Even all the people who'd come up to her afterwards and patted her on the back had been little comfort.

'You were totally brill, Evie.'

'What a fantastic song!'

'Like, how cool were you?'

And most galling of all, 'That was completely amazing! No wonder you got second prize!'

She supposed she knew, deep down, that Paul had deserved to win. You couldn't fault him for niceness either; he'd waited for her to come and collect her things from the changing room and greeted her with a great big wordless bear hug. She'd congratulated him as best she could, and said, 'So I guess you'll be going to the national contest in London now?'

'Looks that way,' he said. 'Scary or what?' But he didn't look very scared, just incredibly excited.

The fact that it couldn't have happened to a nicer person didn't really make it any easier, reflected Evie, sitting on the stairs. It was turning into a seriously bad month generally, what with the whole Dave saga and now this. She kicked at an old fruit gum packet on the bottom step and sighed, resting her face dejectedly in her hands and leaning her elbows on her knees.

'Cheer up, misery guts,' said a relentlessly gleeful voice in her ear. Jade was looming over her.

'Nothing to be cheerful about,' said Evie despondently, hardly bothering to look up.

'Don't talk such drivel,' said Jade. 'Shove over, I can hardly fit in there, can I?'

Evie moved sideways and made a small space on the stair next to her.

'That's more like it,' said Jade, wedging herself between Evie and the wall. 'Why all the gloom and doom? I'd have thought you'd be over the moon, coming second.'

Evie regarded her with scornful disdain. 'What's so good about coming second?'

'What's so good about coming second?' repeated Jade. 'Well, you've made it, haven't you? The world is crammed with people who are famous 'cause they came second! Think Will Young and Gareth Gates. Or everyone who ever went on *Big Brother*. You only gotta be seen and you're famous. All you need is the personality.'

'Yeah, but they were all on telly. I'll never get that far now.'

'Oh, give me a break and stop your whingeing! At least you came second, not third. I didn't hear Vicki bellyaching.'

Evie had the grace to look slightly ashamed. She hadn't thought to find out how Vicki was feeling. She opened her mouth to say something, then remembered that she and Jade were not on speaking terms. 'Anyway, what are you doing here?' she said, suddenly hostile. 'I thought you'd be off partying with your boyfriend.'

'What boyfriend?' said Jade innocently.

'As if you didn't know.'

'Oh, you mean Dave. Although I haven't a clue why you think he's my boyfriend. I tried to tell you in French—'

'What do you take me for, a complete plonker? I saw you. You went back to his place that Saturday when he'd originally been going to spend the evening with me.'

'Yeah, but you gave him the push, didn't you? So. Finders keepers.'

'So now he's with you big time.'

Jade wriggled uncomfortably. 'Not exactly.'

'Let me guess,' said Evie bitterly, 'he got what he wanted, then he dumped you.'

'It wasn't like that at all.'

'What, then? Don't tell me he changed his mind?'

Jade said nothing.

'He *did*? He turned you down?' Evie looked at her with renewed interest.

'That wasn't quite what happened.' Jade shifted her bottom to a more comfortable position on the cold stone. 'He really did intend to get it on with me, 'specially with you coming over all high-minded and everything. But when it came to it—'

'Well?'

'Well, you know how Adam liked him and everything? That conversation you and me had about Adam being gay?'

'As if I'd forget,' said Evie.

'Well, it turns out that Dave's the same. Girls don't do it for him either. All that cracking on to you was a big front. He was just trying to squash his real feelings.'

'What are you talking about? That's just not possible!' said Evie, but even as she spoke she remembered how odd Dave had been with her. How she'd kept having the feeling that he was just going through the motions when they were cuddled up together; as though he was snogging her because it was expected of him.

Jade said, 'I went back to his house, true, but once it got obvious I wasn't really what he wanted, I left. So in the end Adam was the lucky one that night.'

'You mean, he and Adam—?' Was this what Adam had been holding back from her?

'Yeah, he and Adam. Obviously, I don't know all the gory details but I think you can safely assume that they've gone beyond football chat.' Jade was watching Evie's face to see her reaction. 'Hasn't Adam talked to you about it?'

'Not in so many words. But now I see...' Evie pondered for a minute, then said slowly, 'I guess that's what he was on about in his letter about staggering from crisis to crisis and having no power to help himself.' She thought a bit more, then said, 'He's not going to go down that road, I don't think, Jade.'

'Yeah, well, whatever.' Jade examined the bright blue nail on her little finger. 'I'm not one to tell people how they should run their sex lives. Tell you what, though.'

'What?'

'I envy you. You got it made. You got a dad who thinks you're the bee's knees and loads of friends who'll do anything for you. No one really cares what happens to me. Not even my step-mum.'

'That's not true; you know she cares about you. Lots of people care about you.'

'Not like you got, though. Your dad: OK, I know the anorak's a massive drawback, but anyone can see he's proud to bits of you. You got Vicki who's, like, always there when you need someone, and you and Adam go back to the beginning of the world.' She grinned. 'It's in the Bible, innit? In the beginning, Adam and Eve. Not everyone has people like that to love them. It's kind of special too, you being Christians and all that, like there's some kind of spooky extra magic ingredient. As if you all know what life is all about. I wish I could believe like you do.'

'Jade, you make it sound so simple. It really isn't. Half the time I'm not sure if God's actually there at all.'

'Yeah, but deep down it's as if you know someone's looking after you and helping you live the right way and everything. Like, even when your mum died, you never threw yourself off a high building the way I wanted to when my mum went off. It was like you had some kind of extra supply of guts to see you through.' She laughed. 'Makes losing singing contests seem pretty unimportant.'

'I s'pose it does,' said Evie. Then, as an afterthought, 'There's nothing to stop you believing too if you want to.'

'Yeah, but I'm not good enough, am I? You know the kinda things I get up to.'

'It's nothing to do with being good,' said Evie. 'It's just a decision you make and God does the rest. He changes you, makes you into a different person. You just have to be willing for him to do it.'

'Yeah, well. Maybe.' Jade stood up. 'Here's Adam.'

Adam was at the foot of the stairs, slightly red in the face as he struggled with the keyboard and a large box of electrical equipment.

He was bursting with a piece of amazing news. 'I wondered where you were. Thought you'd gone home without me. Guess, what, Eves!'

'No, can't.' She'd had enough guessing games for one day.

'I've just been talking to Johnny Harker and he said my song was so good he wants me to consider writing something for him! Can you imagine? Not with the band, he wants to do some solo work on his own, and thought mine was exactly the sort of music he'd like to do! Me! Writing a song for a proper famous singer! I just can't believe it!'

'Wow,' said Evie in awe.

'And that's not all. Barraclough thinks I should do music as a career, He thinks I've got what it takes. Can you imagine that, old Cloughie, who never listens to anything except Bach or Mozart, thinks I could succeed as a composer? It's all so amazing, Eves.' He paused to draw a breath. 'And much of it is thanks to you, singing my song so well. I'm really sorry you didn't win.'

'No, no, it really doesn't matter. What could be better than your talent being recognised?' Suddenly, amazingly, this was the truth. A thought struck her. 'P'raps this is God's whole new plan for you.'

'Do you really think so?' said Adam excitedly. 'I had the same idea myself. What do you think, Jade?'

Jade shrugged. 'Anything's possible.'

A piece of electric cable fell out of Adam's box onto the floor. 'Pants. Knew that was going to happen. Any chance you could help carry some of this home, Eves?'

Evie got to her feet. ''Course. When have I ever failed you?'

Twelve

It was a particularly busy Friday night in Le Café Rouge. Evie sat at the head of the table with Tom and Adam on either side of her and their parents sat opposite each other at the far end.

'So what's a *paillard de boeuf in a jus de legume* with *pommes sauté*?' asked Adam reading out from an enormous menu. It was too tall to see over the top and he had to lower it sideways to speak.

'Steak and chips,' replied George. 'Roughly, anyway.'

'And *bifteck avec champignons* on a bed of *pommes pont-neuf*?'

'Steak and chips again,' said George.

'OK, what about *tournedos grillé* with *pommes chantilly*?'

'Steak and ch—' began George, but Julie interrupted him. 'Chantilly potatoes are mash not fries.'

'I don't think you'll find they are.'

'Are too. They're done with cheese.'

'Are you sure? Since when have you been an expert on French cooking?'

They began to argue good-naturedly. Tom took the menu from Adam and scrutinised it with determined concentration.

Adam grinned at Evie at their end of the table. 'Like an old married couple.'

She smiled back. 'I know. Reminds me of how he used to be with Mum.'

'Does it hurt?' he asked. 'Seeing them together?'

'No. It's good to see Dad happy again. I thought it might be a bit strange, coming out for a meal on Julie's birthday, remembering how we always made such a fuss of Mum's, but it's OK. It's kind of different, but still nice.'

'Do you think they'll get married?' asked Adam.

'Sure of it. Look at them.' George and Julie had stopped arguing and were holding hands across the table, gazing into each other's eyes in the candlelight.

'So we'll be brother and sister,' said Adam. 'Just like people always think we are anyway.'

'Won't be much different then, will it?' said Evie.

'Might be for Tom.'

'Yeah. I'm not sure how much he wants me for a sister.'

'You'd be surprised,' said Adam. He reduced his voice to a whisper so that Tom wouldn't hear from behind the menu. The restaurant was very full and the background noise made it hard to hear what he was saying. 'Tom thinks a lot of you.'

'How do you know?'

'I can tell. Only yesterday he told me that you had your head screwed on the right way. He's been kinda different the last few days. Not picking fights with me all the time any more.'

'Well, let's hope it lasts,' said Evie with some surprise. She'd had a couple of chats with Tom recently and hadn't been able detect any change in his attitude to Adam, but maybe something Ben had said had got through to him after all. 'You heard about Dave?' she said. 'About what he's doing in London?'

'Yeah, I heard.'

'About him hanging out in the gay scene, pubs and clubs and all that?' she persisted, even though Adam's scowl told her she had touched a raw nerve.

'Yeah, yeah, I heard it all.'

'How do you feel about him now?'

Adam picked a loose piece of wax off the candle. 'It still hurts thinking about it. But I've decided that's not how I want to live. I know it's going to be difficult but it looks as though God's on my case and I've got you and I've got Mum.'

'And my dad too, by the looks of things,' said Evie. 'Anorak and all. And maybe even Tom, in time.'

'Maybe. I'm coming to realise that life's not all about sex. Friends and family are very important too, and God most of all. You're lucky though, Eves, the whole relationship thing isn't so hard for you.'

'That's what you think. I guess the pressures are different, but in the end it's all about not following the world, just like Ben said.'

'Well, we've got each other to help. Tell you what; I'll keep you in line, if you'll do the same for me. Deal?'

'Deal.' They linked little fingers to seal the pact.

Adam reached over to Tom and snatched the menu back from him. 'Oi, loser, gimme that. I haven't finished with it yet.'

Evie sat back in her chair and surveyed the table with satisfaction. She would always miss her mum but it was good to be part of a family again, even if they were a slightly bizarre bunch. And even better to have God watching over it all, helping them over the blips.

It looked as if things might work out OK.

***

Designer Label

'There are so many sides to the Real Me. There's the me who is friends with Sabrina who wants to be trendy and amusing. There's the me who is reliable with Kate and Becky, who wants to be a steady reliable Christian, a support to her friends in times of crisis. There's the me who is trying to be an academic genius to dazzle the teachers. And of course most importantly, there's the me that wants to be gorgeous, witty and wonderful whenever Phil Riley is around.'

Can Charlie manage to be all these people at once? Or is something going to have to give?

ISBN 1 85999 212 9

In the Spotlight

Dan and Jess meet when they are cast in the school panto. Their friendship develops offstage but it's not plain sailing – each has different expectations. Dan finds that being known to have certain beliefs really does put him in the spotlight.

ISBN 1 85999 440 7

Halfway House

When Laura's church is left an old pub in a will, nothing gets in the way of the youth group as they convert it into a drop-in café. Not even attacks by a gang of vandals will stop them from having a place of their own where they can meet.

But when one of the group falls seriously ill they are faced with far greater problems than any of them could have imagined…

…and none of them are prepared when the unthinkable happens.

ISBN 1 85999 556 X

You can buy these books at your local Christian bookshop, or online at www.scriptureunion.org.uk/publishing or call Mail Order direct 08450 706 006